CARTOON
NETWORK

SCOOBY-DOO!
SUPER
CASE
BOOK
II

CARTOON NETWORK

SCOOBY-DOO'S

SUPER

CASE

BOOK II

BY Suzanne Weyn

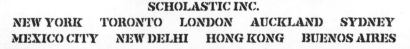

SCHOLASTIC INC.

NEW YORK   TORONTO   LONDON   AUCKLAND   SYDNEY

MEXICO CITY   NEW DELHI   HONG KONG   BUENOS AIRES

No part of this publication may be reproduced in whole or in part, or stored in a retrieval system, or transmitted in any form or by any means, electronic, mechanical, photo-copying, recording, or otherwise, without written permission of the publisher. For information regarding permission, write to Scholastic Inc., Attention: Permissions Department, 557 Broadway, New York, NY 10012.

ISBN 0-439-54605-2

Designed by Louise Bova

12 11 10 9 8 7 6 5 4 3 2 1   4 5 6 7 8 9/0
Printed in the U.S.A.
First printing, May 2004

CONTENTS

THE CASE OF THE ANGRY ORCA 1

THE CASE OF THE VIDEO GAME GHOUL 15

THE CASE OF THE
HOLLYWOOD PHANTOM 26

THE CASE OF THE FLOATING PHANTOM . . .40

THE CASE OF THE PROPHETIC PAINTING . . .59

THE CASE OF THE SCARY SKATER 77

THE CASE OF THE DREADFUL DRAGON 95

THE CASE OF THE
SKATEBOARDING SCAM 113

THE CASE OF THE RIVER RAT 128

THE CASE OF THE BROADWAY BOUNDER . .138

THE CASE OF THE ANGRY ORCA

"**S**cooby! Shaggy! Those little fish are for the dolphins!" Velma cried. "Don't eat them!"

"Like, why should the dolphins have all the fun here at Seven Seas Amusement Park?" Shaggy asked. He popped a small fish into his mouth and tossed one to Scooby-Doo.

"We're not here to have fun," Velma reminded them. "Mystery, Inc. is here to solve a case, remember?"

"I'm trying to forget," Shaggy said, swallowing another tiny fish. "Can't we have a vacation?"

"After we solve this mystery, we can have some fun," Velma told him, smiling.

She headed over to Fred and Daphne, who were feeding the dolphins that swam in a large pool nearby. She started tossing fish to the dolphins, too. "I wonder what the problem is over at the Orca Show," she said.

Fred looked at his watch. "The next show is in five minutes. Let's get over there and find out."

"Okay," Velma agreed. "Let me just use up the last of my fish." She looked for a dolphin to feed. Soon a big set of jaws opened wide. "Here you go," she said, throwing a fish. The jaws snapped shut, and Velma jumped back in surprise. "Scooby!" she shouted. "Get out of that dolphin pool right now." Shaggy was paddling around in there, as well. "Shaggy, you, too. We have to go to the killer whale show over at Orca Stadium."

Shaggy and Scooby splashed out of the tank and joined the rest of the gang. "Orca is another name for killer whale," Velma explained to Shaggy and Scooby.

"This show is Seven Seas Amusement Park's most popular attraction."

The gang got in line and were soon sitting close to a very big tank of salt water. It had glass walls that let them see three huge black-and-white killer whales swimming under the water inside.

"Look! You can watch them on the video screen, too," Daphne said, pointing to the screen mounted over the tank. Underwater cameras filmed the swimming whales for the audience to observe.

The show began with trainers throwing fish to the whales. The whales jumped up and spun in the air, then swam in formation as a group, leaping and gracefully skimming the water. "I don't see any problem here," Fred commented. But just as he spoke, scary music started to play over the sound system — *dumdum-dumdum-dumdum.* It grew louder and faster.

A glowing green orca came crashing through the video screen. It plunged below the water's surface and zoomed back up, making a huge splash. The entire audience was soaked.

The orca hovered in the air, just above the water. "I am King of the Orcas! Leave this place at once, or face your doom!" a deep voice boomed.

The audience did as they were told. They scrambled out of the stadium as fast they could.

Dripping wet, the gang crouched behind a row of seats. They watched as the green killer whale plunged back underwater and disappeared.

As soon as the green orca was gone, the kids ran to the tank. A man with white hair in a diving wet suit joined them. "That's the third video screen that this thing has ruined," he complained, shaking his head. "They cost a fortune to replace. And it's the third show it's ruined, too." He turned to face the gang. "I'm Flip McGill, owner of Seven Seas Amusement Park. I'm the one who phoned you and asked Mystery, Inc. to investigate. I'd call the police, but I don't want to frighten off customers. So far, at least, no one knows about it."

"I hate to tell you this — but folks are about to find out," Daphne said as a woman rushed toward them with a TV camera crew close behind. The woman turned toward the camera. "This is Katie Camrazon here at Seven Seas Amusement Park, where a demon from the deep is bedeviling park goers. And here's the park's owner, Mr. Flip McGill. What's going on?"

Flip McGill faced the camera crew. "It's nothing to worry about, I assure you," he said. "This creature has appeared and . . . and . . . and . . ." Clearly, Flip had no idea what to say next.

Katie Camrazon stepped in front of him. "The owner of the park is speechless with shock," she declared to the camera. "This park is no longer safe for tourists."

The gang looked at one another. They had to do something to help. Daphne stepped up to Katie. "Oh, yes it is," she said. "That's because Mystery, Inc. is on the case. Soon we'll have this mystery all wrapped up."

"This is Katie Camrazon saying, 'You heard it here first,'" Katie told her TV audience. "Mystery, Inc., the teenage sleuths with a reputation for getting to the bottom of every case they encounter, are here at Seven Seas. But can they really unravel such a murky mystery?"

When the cameras were off, Katie Camrazon turned to Flip and the gang and smiled brightly. "This is so great. It's my first really big story, and no other re-porter in town has it. I'll really hit the big time with this!"

"How did you hear about this story?" Velma asked.

Katie scowled at her. "A journalist *never* reveals her sources."

Velma turned to Daphne and whispered, "As if she's such a great journalist — she usually covers fashion shows and society parties."

"Hey, interview me," a handsome young man in a wet suit said as he climbed out of the whale tank. "I want to be on TV. Plus, I know a lot about these killer whales." He gave Flip McGill a dark look. "*Some* people don't understand how much I contribute to this park."

"I told you to leave, Surf!" Flip shouted at the young man. "I fired you. What are you still doing here?"

"The orcas are all upset by that thing. It scared them," Surf explained. "Until you can get rid of that monster, I'm coming back to take care of my buddies, the killer whales."

"Not if I have anything to say about it," Flip said.

"Tell me your story," Katie said to Surf. Surf walked out of the stadium with Katie trailing behind him.

"Why did you fire Surf?" Fred asked.

"He made a million mistakes. He gave the whales the wrong food. Their tanks were never clean enough. He was a total goof-off," Flip explained. "My wife completely spoiled him."

"He's your son?" Velma asked.

Flip nodded. "I'm afraid so."

"I think we'd better take a look around," Fred suggested. "Maybe we can find some clues."

The gang spread out in different directions. Fred and Daphne looked around the tank, Scooby and Shaggy searched for clues in the downstairs area, and Velma talked to two young women who worked with the killer whales. In a half hour, they all returned to the front of the stadium.

"Fred and I found this electric air pump," Daphne reported.

"Like, Scoob and I picked up this thing," Shaggy said, showing them a long strip of green plastic.

"The trainers told me that Surf studied engineering in school, but his father wants him to be a marine biologist who studies underwater life. They've been arguing about it for years," Velma told the gang. "I also learned that Flip is having money problems. He doesn't want to raise the prices, but the tickets he sells aren't earning enough money to feed all the animals."

"I think it's time to set a trap for this angry orca," Fred suggested. "Here's what I have in mind." The gang listened while Fred filled them in on the details of his plan. "Shaggy, we'll need you and Scooby to attract the orca's attention," Fred added.

"Forget it," Shaggy said. "Have you forgotten that they're called *killer* whales?"

"But that's only because they eat other fish and sea animals to survive," Velma said. "Remember when I told you I watched a TV movie about orcas just last month — *Killer Whales: Sweet or Savage?* The answer was that they're really sweet."

"I don't care," Shaggy insisted. "The one we're dealing with is green and hovers in the air."

"Would you do it for a Scooby Snack?" Daphne asked, taking a box of snacks out of her handbag.

Shaggy folded his arms stubbornly and shook his head. Scooby did the same.

Daphne shook the box. "How about a whole *box* of Scooby Snacks?"

Shaggy's eyes lit up enthusiastically as he turned to Scooby. "What do you say, pal?"

"Rokay," Scooby agreed, licking his lips.

Later that afternoon, Scooby and Shaggy were dressed in diving suits with flippers on their feet. They stood on the trainers' platform in the middle of the orca tank. "I just hate impersonating live bait, Scoob," Shaggy whispered.

"Ree, roo," Scooby agreed, nodding.

"We'd better get to work, Mr. Scooby," Shaggy said in a very loud voice. "We should drain this tank of seawater, since Mr. McGill will be closing down this attraction."

The sound system suddenly came on. The scary music they'd heard earlier started to play. "*Dumdum-dumdum-dumdum . . .*"

The green orca splashed up out of the tank, soaking Scooby and Shaggy. "Yikes!" Shaggy cried. Scooby jumped fearfully into Shaggy's arms. A low growl filled the stadium. The green orca hovered in midair.

Fred, Velma, and Daphne rushed out onto the platform. "Ready, set, fire!" Fred shouted. The three of them took out blow guns and fired small darts at the green monster.

Jets of air whooshed out where the darts hit. The green orca crumpled and sank into the tank of water. Fred pulled open a trap door in the platform. "Now to reveal who's behind this mean, green, killer whale machine!" he declared.

Do you think you know who's behind the Case of the Angry Orca? See the next page to find out if you're right!

"**J**inkies! It's Katie Camrazon!" Velma cried as Fred grabbed a hold of the reporter's wrist and pulled her up.

"That's right," Fred said. "When Shaggy and Scooby found that piece of green plastic, it tipped us off that the orca was just a fake. The air pump made us think that it was some kind of inflatable device."

"I remembered watching that TV movie about the orcas last month," Velma added. "And it made us wonder who had a connection in the television business. It was Katie Camrazon, of course. She got a hold of one of the remote-controlled animatronic orcas from the TV special and simply had it painted green. It hovered in the air with a small propeller at the bottom of the robotic orca. She was even able to use the sound track from another movie."

"But why, Katie?" Daphne asked.

"I'll never have a big, important career if I don't have big, important stories to report," Katie said. "So I decided to take matters into my own hands and create one myself."

Flip McGill came out onto the platform. "You cost me a lot of money in lost ticket sales and ruined video screens, Ms. Camrazon," he said.

"I'm sorry," she apologized. "How can I make it up to you?"

Flip thought for a minute. Then he smiled. "You can work with my son, Surf, and help him build more of those robotic animals. Since he's studied engineering, it shouldn't be too hard for him. I want to open a new attraction. The money I make on my robotic animals will help feed and care for my real ones," he said.

"Sure thing," Katie agreed.

"Rooby-rooby-roo!" Scooby cheered.

THE CASE OF THE
ViDEO GAME GHOUL

"**S**haggy! Scooby!" Velma called. "It's time to go."

Shaggy and Scooby kept playing the video games they'd started. They'd been playing for hours at The Video Shack Arcade in the mall, and now the rest of the gang was ready to leave. But Scooby and Shaggy were too involved with their games to even hear Velma talking to them.

"I have Scooby Snacks," Daphne said, shaking a box of the treats. Scooby and Shaggy still didn't stop playing. Daphne turned to Fred and Velma. "This is serious," she said.

"I'll say," Fred agreed.

The sudden sound of an angry crowd distracted them. Outside the arcade, people carried signs. Some read: CLOSE THE ARCADE. Others read: DOWN WITH VIDEO GAMES.

"What's this about?" Fred asked one of the protesters.

"We're with PAVE, Parents Against Video Entertainment," the man explained. "Our children spend too much time here. We can't get them to come home and do homework."

Velma nodded toward Scooby and Shaggy. "We know how that is," she commented.

"We want this place shut down," the PAVE man told her.

"What's going on?" asked a pretty, dark-haired woman. "I'm Rae Gonzalez and I own this arcade. What's the problem?"

"You're ruining our kids!" the PAVE man yelled.

"That's crazy," Rae Gonzalez insisted.

"It's up to parents to limit how long their kids can stay."

The owner of the bookstore next to the arcade walked over to them. "I agree with PAVE. The noise never ends, and it's ruining the business in my antique bookstore. People need quiet to look at the old books."

"You just want my space so you can expand your store, Manny," Rae Gonzalez replied.

"I agree with PAVE, too," said a woman with short gray hair. "I could get a much better tenant in this space."

"Bertie Bucks, you just want to charge more money for this space in your mall," Rae protested. "But you gave me a five-year lease three years ago, when you were desperate to get store owners into this mall. You can't just throw me out now. Besides, the kids love it here. It's a nice, safe place for them to meet their friends."

"Hey! Like, help!" a familiar voice cried.

"Relp!"

The gang turned back toward the arcade game machines. "That was Shaggy and Scooby, but where are they?" Fred asked.

"In here. We're in here!" Shaggy shouted. They followed the sound of his voice to a video game called Ghouls Rule.

"I don't see them," Fred said.

"Right rere!" Scooby yelled.

Fred, Daphne, and Velma looked at the screen of the Ghouls Rule game — and gasped. "Jeepers!" Velma cried. Scooby and Shaggy were *inside* the video game! "How did you get in there?" Velma asked, but Scooby and Shaggy only shrugged and shook their heads, looking as confused as the rest of the gang.

Suddenly, a fiendish laugh echoed from above Fred, Daphne, and Velma. A frightening creature stood on top of the Ghouls Rule video game. It had rotted skin and deep, sunken sockets for eyes. It had long, ragged claws and wore torn clothing. "Raaarrr!" it growled.

Its growl attracted the attention of all the kids in the arcade. They thought it was some kind of show and gathered around it. But the parents from PAVE also saw the creature. They ran into the arcade and grabbed their children, hurrying them out.

When the gang looked again, the video screen was blank and the ghoul was gone.

Daphne turned to Fred and Velma, "We need a plan. We've got to find Scooby and Shaggy!"

Fred nodded. "Velma, you look around the arcade. Daphne and I will search the surrounding stores," he said.

"Will do," Velma agreed as she knelt and picked up a screw from the floor. "Do you know what this came from?" she asked Rae.

Rae studied the screw. "It looks like

the type of screw that keeps the control panel doors shut on the video games," she said.

Velma kept looking around the arcade. "Where does this door lead?" she asked Rae, pulling at a door handle in the ceiling.

"Stairs pull down and they lead to the roof of the mall," Rae explained. "All the stores have them."

"Interesting," Velma commented as she pulled on the door and the stairs came down. She climbed up and found herself on the roof. A cash register receipt blew past her. She reached out and grabbed it. It was from a store in the mall, Electronics Alive, and it was for $800. "This might be important," she said, slipping the receipt into the pocket of her skirt.

She heard a banging coming from a shed on the roof. "Hey, like, get us out of here!" came a cry. It was Shaggy! But when Velma tried to pull the door open, it was locked.

"Are you all right in there?" she called.

"We're fine — just get us out of here!" Shaggy yelled.

"I'll be right back," Velma told him. "I'm going to go downstairs and get some help."

Fred and Daphne were waiting for her at the bottom of the stairs. "Scooby and Shaggy aren't in that video game," Velma told them. "They're locked in a shed on the roof."

"Thank goodness you found them. Look what *we* found," Daphne said. She showed Velma a video film case. "We found it on the floor in front of Manny's bookstore, Manny Pages." Velma showed them the receipt from the electronics store.

The three kids crossed to the Ghouls Rule game. A screw was missing from the side panel. Fred opened up the rest of the panel and they peered inside.

"Well, now what?" Velma asked.

Before anyone could answer her, a

line of sunlight suddenly streamed down from the roof. "There's a hole in the ceiling!" Fred whispered sharply. As soon as he said it, the hole went dark as though someone had covered it again quickly.

Fred ran to the trapdoor and climbed the ladder to the roof. If he was fast enough, he might catch whoever had opened up that hole. But he was only fast enough to hear a door close on the roof.

"Help!" Shaggy shouted from the shed.

Fred leaned close to the door. "You'll have to stay locked up just a little while longer," he told them. "We need your help with a plan."

"As if things aren't already bad enough," Shaggy said with a sigh.

"Ruh-ruh," Scooby agreed sadly.

An hour later, the gang was ready for action. Rae had closed the arcade, so they were alone. Velma stood by the Ghouls Rule game and took out a small tape recorder. She played a recording of kids' voices laughing.

The Ghouls Rule game screen suddenly flashed on. Scooby and Shaggy once again appeared to be in the game, standing on a blue screen. "Come on, like, get us out of here!" Shaggy wailed. "We're hungry!"

"Raarrr!" The Ghoul appeared on top of the video game again. Then, suddenly, the trapdoor opened and a man fell down to the floor. The Ghoul vanished. Fred and Daphne, who'd been waiting on the roof, quickly climbed down the ladder after him. The man got up to run but was tackled by Fred and Daphne.

Do you know who the man is? To find out if you're right, turn the page.

"**m**anny Pages!" Velma cried, running over to help Daphne and Fred. She reached into Manny's jacket pocket and pulled out a set of keys to the shed. "I'll go let Scooby and Shaggy out," she said, climbing the ladder.

"How did you figure it out?" Manny asked.

"Velma found a screw from the video machine and a receipt from an electronics store," Fred explained. "That made us suspicious that someone had been tampering with a game and that some sort of electronic device had been used. Sure enough, we found a closed-circuit camera inside the game. That explained how you put Scooby and Shaggy into the game. They were really in the shed and you were filming them against a blue background."

"You used a video camera to project an image of the Ghoul through that hole in the ceiling," Daphne added. "You went through all that effort just so you could expand your store and get rid of the arcade."

"I would have gotten away with it, too, if it weren't for you meddling kids," Manny snapped, as Scooby and Shaggy came down the stairs with Velma. "And your meddling dog, too," the man added.

Scooby grinned at him. "Rooby-rooby-roo!" he cheered.

THE CASE OF THE HOLLYWOOD PHANTOM

"**T**his is so exciting," Daphne said as they walked onto the movie studio lot in Hollywood, California. "The movie company actually wants to make a motion picture about Mystery, Inc. I wonder who'll play my part."

Scooby-Doo grinned. He was already enjoying the role of celebrity. He wore dark glasses with a long, white, silk scarf.

"This way to Studio A," Fred said as he read a sign in front of him. "Come on, gang."

At Studio A, a low cement building, the gang headed inside to the movie set. The movie company had built the inside of a haunted house. A tall woman in a feathery costume passed by with five doves perched on her arms. About twenty other people walked around, reading scripts.

The kids were greeted by the director, Dino DiWowow. "Ah, the great detectives," he exclaimed. "This will be an exciting movie! We are casting now, searching for actors who will play the parts of four kids from Coolsville who ride around in a groovy van and solve mysteries."

"Rahem," Scooby cleared his throat.

"Oh, yes," Dina DiWowow added, "and their small pony, too."

Scooby looked very insulted. "Like, he's a large dog, not a small pony," Shaggy corrected the director.

"Are you sure?" Dino DiWowow asked the gang.

"Positive," Velma said. "He only *eats* as much as a small pony."

"Very well," said DiWowow. "I have taken the story for my movie from an actual case that Mystery, Inc. solved. I read about it in the newspaper and —" He was interrupted by the sound of a woman screaming.

The gang ran over to the front of the haunted house set. A young actress ran out, pale and shaking. "There's something horrible in there!" she cried. "That house really *is* haunted."

"But it's just a movie set," Daphne said.

"I don't care," the actress said. "I went inside it to get the feel of the character, and a ghost appeared. She blasted me with some kind of energy field and something flew past my head. I'm leaving!"

"Wait!" cried Dino DiWowow. "You were going to read for the part of the beautiful, sophisticated Daphne Blake. I was seriously thinking of giving you the part."

"Forget it!" the young woman said. "This is too scary." Dino DiWowow ran after her, pleading with her to stay.

A young woman with short brown hair and dressed in overalls hurried over to them. "Don't tell me," Velma said. "You're trying out for the part of the brilliant-yet-underappreciated Velma Dinkly."

"No, I'm the underappreciated assistant director, Belinda Bean," she said. "Can I help you?"

"I'd like to see what's inside this haunted house movie set," Fred requested.

"Sure," she agreed. "Help me push the front of the house out of the way and I'll show you." The gang helped her slide away the front panel of the house. Behind it was a creepy front parlor. "This is where the interior scenes will be filmed," she explained.

Scooby sniffed at something on a shabby old-fashioned couch. "Sunflower seeds," Fred noticed. "Don't eat those, Scooby. They might be a clue."

"Maybe this is a clue, too," Daphne said. She'd sat on the old couch and now she pulled something glowing from the cushions. "It looks like a small dog collar, but it glows like those sticks that you snap to make them light up."

The tall woman with the doves walked over to the set. The doves were no longer on her shoulders, but were flying overhead. "Which one of you is Daphne Blake?" she asked.

"That's me," Daphne answered.

The woman stared at her. "I thought you'd be taller," she said.

"This is Tina DiWowow, the director's sister," Belinda Bean said. "She's playing the role of a woman who has a bird act as part of a haunted carnival. It's toward the end of the movie."

Tina DiWowow whistled, and the doves landed on her outstretched arms. "I trained these birds just for the part. I'm a major talent, unlike my brother, who wouldn't know talent if he tripped over it." She walked off, still holding her birds.

"That's true," Belinda agreed. "I should have been the director on this movie, not Dino."

Another scream rang through the movie set. A young woman ran into the parlor. "I was rehearsing the part of Daphne, and this ghost appeared to me. She threw a ball of white energy at me and told me to go — so I'm going!" Still trembling, she started to walk off the set.

"Wait," Fred called to the young woman. "What's stuck to the bottom of your shoe?"

The woman bent down and peeled a piece of white material from her heel. "It must have come from the costume department," she said.

Fred took it from her and put it in his pocket. "Maybe we should have a look around the costume department," he suggested. Belinda Bean told the gang where the costumes were kept, and they went to have a look.

On the way, they were stopped by a man wearing a baseball cap, T-shirt, and jeans. He was with a slim, strawberry-blond woman. "Are you Daphne?" he asked. Daphne nodded and the man scowled. "I thought you'd be shorter," he said.

"What do you know about this movie?" Fred asked.

"Only that I'm going to replace Dino as director, and I'll cast my wife, Gina, as Daphne Blake," the man said. "I'll find a way. You'll soon be hearing a lot about Jerry and Gina Jones. That's us."

Dino DiWowow came down the hall. "Get out of here, you two troublemakers!" he shouted at the Joneses. "I told you I didn't want you here." The couple ran down the hall as the director chased them.

Velma turned to Daphne. "Did you notice that everyone wants to be you and not me?" she asked.

"That's just a coincidence," Daphne said. She turned and saw a sign that read: COSTUMES. "Here it is." They entered a large room with costumes hanging on metal racks. There were shelves with hats, shoes, and all sorts of costume odds and ends.

"It looks like they must have just finished some kind of scary movie," Velma observed as she pushed white gowns on hangers down a rack. "They have all these ghostly looking costumes."

Fred took the scrap of fabric from his pocket. "This fabric is the same as the fabric on these costumes. But none of the gowns seems to be torn or missing a piece."

Scooby sniffed at something in a tall closet. "What is it, pal?" Shaggy asked. Some old shoes tumbled from the top of the closet. Scooby jumped into Shaggy's arms fearfully. A second later, the entire contents of the closet fell out.

But that wasn't all. The gang stared as a glowing white figure emerged from the closet and floated across the room. It shimmered with white energy. "Be gone! Be gone!" it howled. Then it began to toss shining white balls at the gang.

The kids ducked the energy balls, which rose up and returned to the ghost. The gang ran for the door, but it was locked. The ghost kept tossing the balls at them.

"This way!" Velma called, pointing at a laundry chute. The gang jumped down and slid to a landing in a heap of costumes.

"Jinkies, look what I found," Velma said, picking up a note written on a pad. "It was in this pile of dirty costumes." She showed the paper to the others. It read: I'LL SHOW HIM WHO HAS TALENT! "And look at these three strange marks," she pointed out. "It's like a 'V' with a third line in the middle."

"I think it's time to spring a trap," Fred said. "Shaggy, we'll need someone to bring out this Hollywood Phantom."

"And you're thinking that would be me?" Shaggy guessed. "Well think again. I won't do it — too scary!"

"How about you, Scooby?" Daphne asked. "Would you do it for a box of Scooby Snacks?"

"Rokay!" Scooby agreed.

"Hey, no fair!" Shaggy objected. "You didn't even try to bribe me!"

"This is Hollywood, Shaggy," Velma said. "Once you turn down a role, you have to live with your decision."

"Hmumph," Shaggy fumed as he watched Scooby gobble down the yummy treats.

In less than an hour, the trap was set. Scooby was dressed in a red wig and a dress. He sat on the old couch in the haunted house set and pretended he was trying out for the role of Daphne. The rest of the gang crouched low behind the couch, waiting for the phantom to appear.

In minutes, the creature from the costume room rose up on the set. It glowed beneath a field of white. "Be gone!" it howled. "Be gone!" It began tossing its white energy balls at Scooby.

As the balls came hurtling through the air, Velma stood and held up a cage with its door wide open. Each of the balls changed direction and flew right into the cage.

Daphne and Fred jumped up and grabbed hold of the bottom of the phantom. But the phantom rose into the air, taking them up with it! Scooby and Shaggy held onto Fred's and Daphne's feet and yanked them down. They fell into a pile on the floor, phantom and all.

"Now let's see who this phantom is," Fred said as he grabbed hold of the white ghost costume.

Do you know who's behind the Hollywood Phantom? See the next page to find out if you are right.

"It's Tina DiWowow!" Fred announced, "just as we thought."

"How did you know?" she asked.

"You spilled those unsalted sunflower seeds on the couch," Velma said. "That was something your doves would have liked. One of your doves also lost its little glowing collar, which we found." She reached into the cage and pulled out one of the glowing balls of energy. It was really a dove wearing a glowing collar, with white material wrapped around it. "None of the ghost costumes was cut because you took an entire costume and cut it up. We put sunflower seeds in this cage to make all the birds fly into it."

"You were able to rise and float around because the whole movie set is full of cables and wires for special effects," Fred continued. "Just now, you were hooked to a line, and it was strong enough to pull up Daphne and me with it, although it couldn't hold the weight when Scooby and Shaggy hopped on, too."

"The clue that really gave you away was the note we found in the costume laundry room," Velma added. "That note could have been written by any of the suspects, but one of your doves stepped on it and left a bird track on the paper."

Dino DiWowow and Belinda Bean rushed up to them. "Why would you go to so much work to cause all this trouble?" Dino DiWowow asked his sister.

"I wanted the part of Daphne Blake," she shouted. "I'm your sister. Don't you think you could give me a part in a movie, just once?"

"But you have no talent," Dino Di-Wowow said.

"So what?" she asked. "I deserve more than to be the carnival girl."

"Well, now you are not even the carnival girl," Dino DiWowow told her. "You're fired!"

Tina DiWowow threw her phantom costume at her brother. "Oh, yeah? I'm telling

Mom!" She stormed past him, but Dino ran after her.

"No! Don't do that!" he pleaded.

"Maybe their mom will ground him and I'll get to direct the picture," Belinda Bean said hopefully. She looked at Scooby. "And I'll let *you* play the role of Daphne Blake!"

"Rooby-rooby-roo!" Scooby shouted.

"Jeepers! Look at all these hot air balloons," Velma said as the Mystery Machine came to a stop on a flat, grassy field. "INTERNATIONAL HOT AIR BALLOON FESTIVAL," she read on a large sign in the field. "I can't wait to go up in one of them."

"Do you know how to work one?" Daphne asked, as the gang climbed out of the van.

"Well, I've been researching it on my laptop computer, and it seems pretty simple," Velma replied. "Hot air causes the balloon to go up. Letting out hot air makes it come down."

"We have a mystery to solve before we have time to go riding around in balloons," Fred reminded them. "That's why we're here, after all."

"I was hoping we were here to sample the food at all these booths," Shaggy said. He sniffed the delicious smells coming from the fairgrounds, next to the large balloons. There were also rides, and even a little petting zoo. "Hey, where's Scoob?" he asked.

"Scooby-Doo, where are you?" Velma called.

"There he is," Shaggy said, pointing. "He beat me to the food! He's over by the booths."

Scooby-Doo peeked out from behind a big puff of pink. "Rotton randy," he said, licking his lips.

A bald man in a tie-dyed T-shirt hurried to the gang. "You must be Mystery, Inc.," he said. "I'm so glad you came. I'm Willie Flay, the organizer of this fair, and I really need your help."

"What's up?" Fred asked.

"None of these air balloons are up.

That's my problem. But if I tell you my story, you probably won't believe me," Willie said.

"Oh, you'd be surprised what we'd believe," Shaggy said.

"That's for sure," Daphne agreed.

"Maybe it would be better if I brought you up in a balloon and showed you," Willie said. He led the gang toward an orange-and-yellow balloon. Everyone climbed in, and Willie turned a dial similar to one on a stove. "Up we go!" he said, pulling in the sandbags that weighed down the balloon.

The balloon slowly rose high into the air. "Jeepers," Velma said. "This is super!" Soon they were overlooking the entire countryside.

"What is it you wanted to show us?" Fred asked.

"Wait a few minutes," Willie replied.

A red-and-purple air balloon appeared on the horizon. At first, it was just a tiny dot in the distance, but it quickly floated over to them. "No one is inside the basket," Daphne realized, when the balloon was several yards away.

"It looks that way," Willie agreed.

At that moment, though, a creature with a hideous face leaped up from inside the basket of the other balloon. Its skin was purple and bumpy, and it had bulging eyes and wild green hair. Although it was small, it's arms were extremely long.

"Rikes!" Scooby yelled.

"Double yikes!" Shaggy added as the creature leaped across the air and landed on their basket, letting out a high-pitched scream. It was so loud that it made Scooby cover his sound-sensitive dog ears.

The creature jumped down into the basket. The gang swatted at it as it scurried frantically around. In a minute it went back over the side of the basket and disappeared. The red-and-purple air balloon sailed away as quickly as it had appeared.

"That creature attacks any air balloon that goes up," Willie told them. "That's why all the balloons are on the ground right now. The balloonists are all too frightened to go up. One of them was so scared by that creature that he jumped out of his balloon. Luckily it hadn't gone up too high yet, but he still broke his leg."

"Where are Shaggy and Scooby?" Daphne asked.

"Like, here we are," Shaggy called in a small, scared voice. Fred, Daphne, and Velma looked up and saw them peering down from the top of the balloon. "We can't get down."

"They must have climbed up there to get away from the creature," Velma figured. "It *was* pretty scary."

"Hold on tight! I'm taking us down," Willie shouted up to Scooby and Shaggy.

He turned a dial and the balloon began to descend slowly. "If I don't stop this creature, my festival will be ruined. I spent a lot of money on this festival, and I owe a lot of people money, too. I'll be ruined if the festival is a flop."

"Can you think of anyone who might want to cause trouble for you?" Fred asked.

Willie thought a moment, then shook his head. "No."

Once they were on the ground, Scooby and Shaggy crawled down from the top of the balloon. "Zoinks! That was one creepy creep," Shaggy said.

"A reepy reep," Scooby agreed.

"We should split up and see what we can find out," Fred suggested. Fred and Daphne went over to the petting zoo, while Velma, Scooby, and Shaggy headed for the food booths.

Velma stopped to talk to a man who ran the Ferris wheel. "I heard about that high-flying monster," he said. "This used to be a peaceful area, but now it seems something bad happens all the time!"

"What else happened?" she asked him.

"Don't you read the paper?" he asked.

"Hey! Get us off this thing!" a panicked voice yelled from the merry-go-round nearby. It was Shaggy! The merry-go-round was zooming around faster and faster — and Scooby and Shaggy were on it!

Velma looked for help, but no one was around to shut it off. The merry-go-round spun so fast that Scooby and Shaggy flew off, spinning like tops across the fairgrounds.

"Scooby! Shaggy!" Velma cried, running after them. The two of them stopped spinning when they banged into the front of a pizza stand. "Are you okay?" Velma asked.

"Oh, the agony," Shaggy wailed. "My stomach feels all spun around." He lifted pained eyes to the pizza stand above him. "A slice of pizza might relieve my misery."

"Reah, a rice of rizza," Scooby agreed, nodding and licking his lips.

Velma rolled her eyes. "Oh, you guys! All right." She stood in front of the booth's window and looked in. The man behind the counter was reading the paper and watching the news on a small black-and-white TV. Velma waited a few minutes, but he didn't look up. "Ahem!" Velma cleared her throat to get his attention.

He glanced up from his paper. "Whaddya want?" he snapped.

"This *is* a pizza stand, isn't it?" Velma replied.

"Yeah, yeah, yeah," the man muttered. He reached into a steel refrigerator, took out a piece of pizza wrapped in a clear cellophane bag, and tossed it on the counter. "One dollar," he barked.

"This is frozen!" Velma pointed out indignantly.

"Troublemaker!" the man yelled, and slammed the shutters on the booth's window shut.

Velma blinked hard. "What was that about?" she asked.

Shaggy reached up and took the frozen, wrapped pizza from her. "That's okay," he said. "I'll manage to force it down somehow."

Shaggy was trying to open the bag when a long tongue reached out and wrapped around it. "Scooby!" Shaggy shouted. But it was too late. Scooby-Doo swallowed the frozen pizza, bag and all!

Scooby covered his mouth and chuckled mischievously. "Re-reh-reh-reh!"

"Come on you two, stop clowning around," Velma scolded. "We have a mystery to solve!" They headed back to find the Ferris wheel operator. Velma wanted to ask him what he'd meant when he said bad things had been happening. But when they got there, the Ferris wheel was shut down. So they headed to the hot air balloon field and met up with Daphne and Fred. "Did you discover anything?" Velma asked.

"Just this," Daphne said, holding up a scrap of paper with the letters B-A-R written on it. "We found it at the petting zoo."

"I don't know why you think that's important," Fred said.

"I don't know," Daphne admitted. "It just reminds of something I've seen before."

"Maybe you'll figure it out over supper," Shaggy suggested. "You have to feed the brain, you know."

Fred looked at the setting sun. "We'd better go get some motel rooms," he said.

The gang piled back into the Mystery Machine, but a woman on a motorcycle zoomed up alongside them before Fred could start the engine. She rapped on the driver's-side window and Fred rolled it down. "Are you Mystery, Inc.?" she asked. Fred nodded. "I have to talk to you," she went on. "This festival is ruining the environment. All these people bring their cars and pollute. You have to stop them!"

Willie Flay came running over. "Get out of here!" he yelled at the woman.

"You have to catch me first!" she said as she kicked the starter of her motorcycle and zoomed off into the middle of the field.

"Who was that?" Fred asked Willie.

"That's my sister, Frannie," Willie replied. "She gets on my case about the festival every year."

"I see," Fred said. The gang said goodbye to Willie and drove to a nearby motel. After they freshened up, they went to a local diner. Scooby and Shaggy decided to have the veggie-burger platter and ate five helpings each.

"At least the service is better here than at that pizza booth," Velma commented. "That pizza guy had no idea what he was doing, and he was so rude."

That night, Velma sat up in bed, checking the Internet on her laptop computer. She was searching for recent stories in the local paper. "The Ferris wheel guy told me that something bad had been going on lately. I want to find out what he was talking about," she explained to Daphne.

"Find anything?" Daphne asked.

"Maybe so," Velma replied. "I just found a story about how a circus train was robbed last week. Three men took all the money the circus had earned and even set loose some of the circus animals."

"What's the name of the circus?" Daphne asked.

"The Barnabus Kelly Circus."

Daphne nodded. "We saw a sign advertising their circus when we drove into town," she remembered. "Did they get away with it?"

"It says the police chased them into the hot air balloon field. The men took a balloon and escaped," Velma said, reading the laptop monitor. She yawned, shut off the computer, and removed her glasses. "I'm going to sleep. Good night."

Some time around dawn, Velma was awakened by warm breath on her hand. "Scooby, how did you get in here?" she mumbled in her sleep. She patted him on the head.

Her eyes snapped open, though, when Daphne let out a piercing scream from the other twin bed. Velma fumbled on the night table for her glasses. As soon as she'd put them on, she saw that the creepy purple creature was standing between their beds. With a shrill scream, it jumped up onto the foot of Velma's bed, then leaped over to Daphne's bed. It went back and forth with powerful leaps.

Velma and Daphne leaped up and began swatting it with their pillows. The creature screamed again, and seemed to fly across the room. It ducked out the open window. Daphne and Velma raced outside to see where it went. Scooby, Shaggy, and Fred met them in front of the motel. "What's the racket?" Fred asked.

"The creature was in our room," Daphne told him. "He just opened the window and came right in."

"Or someone opened it for him," Velma said as she studied the open window. There was a very human-looking, greasy, black thumbprint on the windowsill.

"The sun's nearly up," Fred observed. "I think we should get over to the balloon field and set a trap for our creepy creature."

A half hour later, Scooby and Shaggy were in a hot air balloon and rising fast. "How come we're always the bait, huh, Scoob?" Shaggy complained. Scooby shrugged as he stuffed his mouth with Scooby Snacks from the box that Daphne had used to bribe him.

They hovered in the air until the red-and-purple balloon appeared in the sky. They let a strong breeze carry them closer to it. The purple creature appeared on the edge of the basket. It swung on the ropes of the balloon, then hung off the end by one hand.

"Get ready, Scoob," Shaggy said. "We're about to be boarded!"

As he spoke, the creature leaped across the air and landed on their balloon. "Now, Scoob!" Shaggy shouted.

Scooby-Doo stuck his nose into a burlap bag and pulled out a thick wad of money. The creature started screaming and grabbed at the money. Scooby scrambled up onto the balloon, and the creature raced right up after him.

Scooby got on his wobbling hind legs and held up the money. He waved it in the air. "Rome and ret rit!" he called to the creature. Then he snapped the rubber band that bound the money together and tossed the money in the air. It blew around them in a million directions.

A figure covered with a black blanket jumped up from inside the red-and-purple balloon. Two arms reached out, trying to grab the falling money.

Meanwhile, the creature leaped at Scooby, knocking him backward. Scooby held on to the creature as he fell off the top of the balloon. They tumbled through the air!

"Scooby!" Shaggy yelled, leaning out of the balloon. "Oh, no! This is awful!"

Scooby and the phantom tumbled over and over. Soon they would hit the ground. But a strong hand reached out and grabbed Scooby's leg. Fred pulled Scooby and the creature into the balloon he, Daphne, and Velma had come up in.

The red-and-purple balloon blew alongside them. Scooby reached out and grabbed onto it. Then an orange-and-yellow balloon came up on the other side of the red-and-purple balloon. Willie Flay and two police officers were inside.

Fred reached across the baskets and into the red-and-purple balloon. He took hold of the black blanket and began to pull it off the person hiding underneath. "Now we'll discover who's behind this creature," he said.

Do you think you know who's behind the mystery of the Floating Phantom? See the next page to find out if you're right!

"It's the guy from the pizza booth!" Velma cried when Fred pulled up the blanket.

"And our floating phantom is a chimp!" Daphne said as she removed the creature's mask.

"This pizza guy is one of the thieves who robbed that circus train," the police officer said. "He's Bart Robbins, a known robber."

"I just wanted my loot back," Bart Robbins snarled. "I tossed it into one of the balloon baskets when I was running from the cops. I had to frighten the people away from their balloons until I could find the money. That's when I had the idea to use the chimp I sprung from the circus. I dressed up the chimp to scare anyone who went up in a balloon. I even trained him to look for the money. It must have been in your balloon. Now you've thrown it all away."

"We figured you were the robber when you didn't know anything about pizza,"

Velma said. "You tried to scare us away by speeding up the merry-go-round and by sending your chimp into our motel room."

"We figured the robber from the circus was behind this when we found that piece of paper marked BAR for Barnabus Kelly Circus," Daphne added.

"Yeah, and I would have gotten away with it, too, if it weren't for you meddling kids. You threw all that money away."

"Not exactly," Fred said. One of the dollars floated past him and he snapped it up. "This is board game money," he said. "We threw it just to force you to reveal yourself."

Right then, Shaggy's balloon raced by, blown by a strong wind. "Hey, how do you stop this thing?" he shouted.

Velma and Daphne laughed. "We'll be right there, Shaggy," Fred called.

"Rooby-rooby-roo!" Scooby cheered.

Fred parked the Mystery Machine in front of the City Art Museum. "Here we are," he said, shutting off the engine.

"Like, I thought we were having lunch first," Shaggy complained from the backseat.

"Reah, runch rirst," Scooby-Doo agreed, rubbing his belly.

Daphne, sitting beside Fred, turned to face the backseat. "Sorry, guys. The director of this museum, Julia Jerome, said we just had to come and see a certain painting right away. She told me there's something very mysterious about it."

"Uh-oh," Shaggy said. "Do you mean mysterious as in a mystery plus us?"

"I'm afraid so," Velma said. She sat beside him, looking at the screen of her laptop computer. "I'm researching the painting on the Internet right now. It was done by a Mexican painter named Maria Comengo. She's very famous in Mexico. Most of her paintings show magicians, since she was a magician's assistant as a young woman. But this painting is different. It's called *Man in a Museum.*"

"Let's go see what this is about," Fred suggested. They got out and went up wide stairs to the large stone building. There were thick pillars and fountains in front.

When they got to the top of the stairs, Shaggy gasped. "Scooby's disappeared!" he shouted. "The curse of the mysterious painting has already started!"

"You mean the curse of the silly dog has already started," Velma said, pointing at one of the fountains. Scooby stood in the middle of it, balanced on one foot, and spraying water out of his mouth like a fountain. The gang laughed and Scooby snickered, accidentally spraying them all with water.

"Hey, come on," Daphne said, shaking water from her hair. "We have to seem like serious detectives. The museum director wants to hire Mystery, Inc. to solve some kind of case."

"We may be all wet," Fred said, "but there's no case we can't solve."

As soon as they went into the grand, high-ceilinged museum, they were met by an attractive woman in a business suit. "You must be Mystery, Inc.," she said. "I'm Julia Jerome. Come right this way, and I'll show you the painting." They followed her across a marble lobby and down a dimly lit hallway. She stopped in front of a painting and drew in a sharp breath. "It's happened again!" she cried.

"What's happened?" Daphne asked.

"The painting has changed," she explained. "When I first got the Maria

Comengo painting, it showed a man in a long coat with a cap walking into this museum. Then the next day, the painting had somehow changed. It showed him walking toward the part of the museum where we display our ancient Roman statues. See all those white marble statues of men wearing Roman togas? Now it shows the man taking a big mallet from inside his jacket."

Velma wiped off her glasses and studied the painting. "That's a mallet all right. I wonder what he plans to do with it."

"What I want to know is how the painting is changing," Fred said. "Who could be doing this?"

A man stepped out of the shadows behind them. He was slim and tall with spiky hair and very thick glasses. "My mother is changing these paintings with her mind," he proclaimed.

"This is Igor Comengo, the painter's son," Julia introduced the man. "He sold us this painting done by his late mother."

"Late?" Velma asked.

"Sí," said Igor. "Mama fell into a vat of orange paint and died last week. But she speaks to us now from beyond the grave."

"Yikes! Like, what's she trying to say?" Shaggy asked.

Igor stepped up dramatically toward the painting. "It's in the painting! She's the one who is changing it. Watch the painting and you will learn what Mama is trying to say. I'm sure of it!" He turned and walked off down the hallway.

"Igor, come back," Julia called as she followed him down the hall. "What do you think she's trying to tell us?"

"She's trying to tell us she never had any talent to begin with!" said a short, muscular man who had walked toward them. He wore a T-shirt, jeans, and a beret on his shiny bald head. Under his arm he carried a large, flat, canvas case.

"That's Paulo Licastro," Daphne whispered to the gang. "He's one of the greatest artists in the world."

"This Comengo painting is trash!" he went on.

"Did you know the artist?" Velma asked.

"Know her!" Paulo cried. "Know her! I asked her to marry me, but she turned me down. Imagine turning down the great Paulo Licastro! She said I didn't respect her art — and, of course, I don't. But I loved her." He reached into his case and pulled out a portrait of a pretty woman with large, dark eyes. "I am giving the museum this portrait that I painted of her. Even though it's worth a fortune, I don't want it anymore. The memories are too painful."

"I read that you were donating this painting," Velma said. "Why aren't there lots of reporters here to write about it?"

"I told them I would be here *next* week. I said it to confuse them," Paulo explained. "I don't want everyone staring at me when I have a broken heart."

He took a painting off the wall and hung the portrait of Maria Comengo in its place. As he did this, Julia Jerome hurried back down the hall with a thin, nervous woman. "Oh, Paulo, you've brought the painting. How marvelous!"

"Everything I do is marvelous," Paulo replied.

"That's so true!" the woman agreed.

"This is Arta Splore," Julia told them. "She's an art expert. I've brought her in to tell me if this painting is a genuine work by Comengo."

Arta Splore took out a magnifying glass and slowly inspected every inch of the painting. "Well?" Julia asked. "Did Maria Comengo paint this?"

Arta Splore thought for a moment. She stared at the painting from the left side, then she moved to the right and stared at it some more. The gang watched her, waiting for her reply. "Yes!" she said at last. "Yes! I can tell from the brush strokes that this is the genuine work of Comengo. And no one else uses blues and grays the way she does."

"That means Maria Comengo really *is* trying to tell us something from beyond the grave," Julia said. "How else could this painting keep changing? Come, Ms. Splore, I'll walk you out."

When they'd gone, Fred, Velma, and Daphne looked at one another. "Where are Scooby and Shaggy?" Fred asked. They looked all around, but the two of them were gone.

"Wait!" Velma said. "I hear something."
Slurp!
They followed the sound around a corner. There they found Shaggy and Scooby staring up at a painting of a bowl of fruit. Scooby was licking a painted apple! "Stop that!" Fred cried. "Do you want to get us thrown out of here?"

"Sorry, but we're just, like, so hungry," Shaggy said as he leaned against the wall, pretending to faint. Then he reached out and grabbed Velma's arm. "If I don't get food soon, I'll just waste away," he said.

At that moment, they heard a terrified scream. "It's coming from the hall with the painting," Velma said. They raced toward the sound.

Julia was standing by the painting, trembling with fear. "I saw him!" she cried, "the man in the painting, the one with the cap and long coat. He was coming toward me down the hall — and then he just disappeared!"

"And look!" Daphne cried, pointing to the painting. "The painting has changed again!" The painting now showed the man smashing one of the Roman statues. It was the statue of a man in a toga with his dog.

"Oh! I can barely stand to view that scene," Julia Jerome said. "Those statues are historical treasures. They're irreplaceable!"

"Well, now we know what she's trying

to tell us," Igor Comengo said, returning. "Obviously this is a warning that someone is going to harm a statue in the Ancient History collection."

Paulo Licastro stepped forward, and Igor gasped. "Paulo!" he cried, obviously surprised to see him.

"Have we met?" Paulo Licastro asked.

"No . . . uh . . . no," Igor stammered. "But you are world famous. Everyone knows you."

"True," Paulo agreed.

Suddenly the lights in the museum began to flicker. An unearthly female voice filled the hallway. "Tonight at ten o'clock. Be ready!" Then the lights went back on.

"Did that sound like your mother?" Velma asked Igor.

He nodded. "Exactly."

"That was her voice. It's true," Paulo added.

"If this is a warning from beyond the grave, we'd better take it seriously," Julia Jerome said. "I'm going to alert security and have them put all their attention on the Roman section. We'll be waiting tonight to make sure nothing happens. In fact, I'm going over there right now."

When they'd all left, the gang stayed behind by the painting. "I think it's time to make a plan," Fred said. In a low voice, he told them what he had in mind. "Shaggy, we'll need you and Scooby to create . . ."

"A diversion?" Shaggy guessed.

"Well . . . at least some confusion," Fred replied.

That night, at ten minutes before ten o'clock, the museum was nearly empty. The only people there were Julia Jerome, the museum security guards, and Mystery, Inc.

The lights were off in the Ancient History hall, and security guards were hidden in the shadows. They were waiting for the man with the long coat and cap to show up.

Velma crouched in a dark corner and spoke softly to Fred on her two-way radio. "Shaggy and Scooby are in place," she reported. Then she saw a tall figure enter. "He's here! Get ready."

Velma watched anxiously as the man approached the ancient Roman statue of a man with a dog. He reached into his coat and — just as they had seen him do in the painting — he took out a mallet. He raised it, as if he was about the strike the statue, when . . .

The statue leaped to life and jumped on him, both the ancient Roman and his dog. It was Scooby and Shaggy posing as statues! They chased him around the other statues.

Velma snapped on the lights and joined them. The security guards jumped out of hiding, but the man was fast. He hit the light switch, plunging them all into darkness again. Then he darted out of the hall.

The guards and Velma chased him into the lobby. They found the long coat and cap on the floor. A guard snapped them up. "I'll check down this hall," he said, walking toward the hall with the Comengo painting. "The rest of you split up and check the other halls."

Shaggy and Scooby caught up with Velma. "Come on," she said. The three of them raced after the guard who had picked up the coat and cap. They got to the hall just in time to see the guard grab a painting off the wall and cover it with the coat. As he started to run again, he stumbled over a velvet cord stretched across the hall.

"Got ya!" Fred said as he stepped out of hiding.

Daphne and Julia Jerome came out from the other side. Julia ran to get the painting. "It's the Licastro painting of Maria Comengo!" she cried.

Fred helped the security guard to his feet. "And this isn't really a security guard," he said.

Julia stared at the man. His cap had fallen off and she could see who he really was. "Igor Comengo!" she cried in surprise.

"Close," Fred said. "But not quite." He reached out to pull off the guard's wig and glasses.

Do you know who is behind this painterly caper? See the next page to find out if you're right!

"It's Maria Comengo!" Fred announced. When he lifted off the wig of spiky hair, long dark curls tumbled out. Removing the thick glasses revealed a set of shining dark eyes.

"She's not dead, after all!" Daphne said. "In fact, she's been here all along, posing as her own son."

"There is no such person as Igor Comengo," Velma added. "My Internet research revealed that Maria Comengo has no children."

"I don't understand," Julia said. "What's this all about?"

"This is *my* painting!" Maria said stubbornly. "It should have been mine. That vain, conceited Paulo Licastro said he would give it me. Then, when I refused his marriage proposal, he took it back. Do you know what an honor it is to have your portrait painted by Paulo Licastro?"

"Not to mention that the painting is worth millions," Daphne said.

"That, too," Maria admitted. "But that was not the reason I did this. All I care about is art. I had to find some way to get this painting."

"So you created a phony mystery that would cause security to focus all its attention in the wrong place. It was very clever, the way you faked your own death and released the story that you had died. After that, you painted this series of paintings and then, posing as Igor, you switched the paintings whenever you had the chance," Velma explained.

"Where did you keep them?" Julia asked.

Fred opened a small storage closet on the opposite wall. "They were right here. And it was this closet Maria disappeared into today when she posed as the man in the long coat and cap," Fred explained. He took a tape recorder out of the closet. "This tape recorder was set on a timer. That's how Maria made the eerie announcement we heard today."

"Tonight, Maria posed as that character again, but wore a guard's uniform under her coat," Velma continued. "She was going to walk out of here with the painting under her jacket and no one would have known who took it."

"I would have gotten away with it, too, if it weren't for you interfering kids!" Maria shouted at them. "How did you figure it out?"

"I became suspicious when I learned there was no real Igor Comengo," Velma said. "Then, later, when Igor seemed to know Paulo Licastro, I knew something strange was going on."

"And the fact that Arta Splore said these were real Comengos told us that you must still be alive," Daphne went on.

"Velma's research also revealed that you were once a magician's assistant," Fred said. "Everyone knows that misdirection is a magician's tool. They tell the audience to look one way, while the trick is performed somewhere else. That's what you did here. You made everyone believe there would be trouble in the Ancient History hall, while the real theft would take place right here."

Julia took the Licastro painting from Maria, and the security guards walked her out. "Thanks, kids," Julia said.

"Don't mention it," Fred said. "It's what we do."

"Reah," Scooby agreed. "Rit's rhat re Rooby-rooby-roo!"

THE CASE OF THE
SCARY SKATER

"**L**eap into my arms, Scoob!" Shaggy instructed. He held out his arms as Scooby-Doo flung himself through the air. "Ooph!" Shaggy staggered backward when Scooby landed in his arms.

Fred, Velma, and Daphne clapped. They stood in front of the arena where the Grand National Figure Skating Competition was being held. "Way to go, guys," Velma said. "Now if you could just skate, you'd be ready to compete in the Grand Championship."

"Who says we can't skate?" Shaggy asked. He and Scooby slid along on the cement as if they were skating.

"It's not as easy when you're wearing skates," Daphne mentioned, giggling.

"Let's go in and see why the owner of this arena called for our help," Fred suggested. They walked in the front door and into the large arena. On the ice, contestants were practicing for the upcoming competition.

"Jeepers, they're talented," Velma commented as she watched the skaters spin and leap through the air. "Some of my favorite skaters are competing." She watched a female skater named Jenny Jumps, an Olympic gold medalist, perform a triple axel jump and land lightly on the ice.

Suddenly, the lights in the arena began to flicker. All the skaters stopped. They couldn't move their feet. It was as if they were glued to the ice.

Then the arena went black. Suddenly, a single spotlight shined down in the center of the rink. A lone figure wearing a black tuxedo skated into it. His face was painted white with black lips, and his eyes were lined with black. His wild black hair stuck out in all directions. He skated around the other skaters as they strained to move their feet. He laughed wildly, then rose into the air and disappeared into the darkness.

Immediately, the lights came back on and the skaters were able to move again. Talking excitedly, they skated off the ice.

"Well, I guess we know what the problem is," Fred said.

"Yeah. That scary skater is really terrifying," Daphne said. "We should find the owner of this place and hear what he has to say."

"That would be me," said a tall, athletic man with wavy white hair. "I'm Icy Blades. That scary skater showed up last night for the first time."

"Do you have any idea how he stops the skaters from moving?" Fred asked.

"Not a clue," Icy replied.

Jenny Jumps joined them. "Icy, you

have to do something about this," she said. "I can't practice under these conditions. This competition means everything to me. My world ranking is at stake."

"I'm sorry, Jenny. I'm baffled by all this. That's why I've hired the Mystery, Inc. detective agency to figure out what's going on," Icy told her.

"You were out there," Velma said. "Why couldn't you move your feet?"

"It was as if they were made of stone," Jenny replied. "I could bend my knees but my feet were stuck to the spot."

Jenny turned back to Icy. "If that lunatic comes back, I'm calling my lawyers. I'll sue you for ruining my chances at this competition," she threatened. Then she stormed away.

As they watched her go, the gang became aware of a short, heavy man talking on a cell phone. "Yes. Yes. It was wonderful. They were all terrified. I loved every minute of it," he said to someone on the other end of the line.

Icy charged over and grabbed his arm. The man dropped the cell phone in surprise. "What do you know about this?" Icy demanded angrily.

The man glared up at Icy. "Unhand me, you goon," he insisted. Icy let him go, and the man rubbed his arm. "I only know that you and this entire sport are getting what you deserve. It serves you all right. They'll remember this as the Haunted Championship." The man turned on his heel and marched off.

Icy went red with rage and raised a fist at the man. "Why, I ought to . . ."

Fred and Daphne took hold of his raised arm and pulled him away. "Who is that guy?" Fred asked.

"He's Los Korz," Icy told them. "He was an international judge, but was banned from judging last year because he was caught taking bribes. He hates skating now, but he shows up at all the competitions."

"Is there any chance we can get out

there on the ice ourselves, to see what's going on?" Daphne asked.

"I'd say you could go right now," Icy said. "It doesn't look as if anyone wants to practice out there anymore."

The gang sat down and put on their skates. One by one, they stepped out onto the ice.

"Jinkies!" Velma cried, swinging her arms wildly to keep her balance. "I haven't done this in a while."

Scooby and Shaggy fell down, but they didn't seem to care. They had fun sliding all over the rink on their stomachs and rear ends. "Like, look at me, Scoob!" Shaggy called. He slid on his stomach and flapped his arms. "I'm a seal sliding across an iceberg!"

Scooby responded by showing off with a trick of his own. He bounced on his tail, spun upside down, and then landed on his tail again. "Way to go for the gold, Scoob!" Shaggy cheered.

Fred looked up and spied a giant disco

ball twirling above the rink. "What's that used for?" he called to Icy, who sat in the bleachers.

"It's for special effects," Icy answered.

The gang skated a few minutes longer. Daphne did graceful spins. "I studied figure skating," she explained.

"I wish I had," Velma said, still struggling to keep from falling.

"I learned to skate so I could play ice hockey," Fred said as he raced around the rink.

Suddenly the lights flashed again. "Roh-no!" Scooby said as a circle of light appeared and the Scary Skater appeared on the ice again. Scooby felt a strong, invisible force pull his dog tag down to the ice. He lay stuck, with his head held down.

The Scary Skater zoomed around the rest of the gang. All of them were frozen where they stood.

The Scary Skater circled Daphne and took out a pair of scissors. He snipped the laces of her skates open, then lifted her out of them. In a second, he was rising into the air with Daphne in his arms. She struggled, but he held on tight. The rest of the gang was unable to help her. Together, Daphne and the Scary Skater spun to the ceiling and disappeared.

The lights turned back on, and suddenly, the gang could move again. "Scooby's down!" Velma noticed, skating over to him. But Scooby was able to lift his head again by the time she reached him. Velma looked at his dog tag. "Hmm," she said. "This is made of steel, isn't it?"

Fred skated to join them, spraying ice as he stopped. "We've got to find Daphne." He looked up. "Let's get up to those catwalks and find out where they lead."

Velma, Fred, Scooby, and Shaggy found a metal staircase leading to the top of the arena. Up there, they could access the series of metal catwalks. Shaggy bent down and picked up a piece of paper. "Could this be a clue?" he asked.

Fred and Velma studied the paper. "It's a receipt for that disco ball over there," Velma said. "According to the date here, it was purchased just three days ago."

"Let's keep exploring up here," Fred said. "Maybe one of these catwalks will lead us to Daphne."

"Hey, Scooby," Velma said. "I think Daphne has a few Scooby Snacks in her pocket. Maybe you could follow the scent of Scooby Snacks and find her."

Scooby sniffed the air with his super-sensitive nose and caught the scent of a Scooby Snack. He followed it up a cat-walk, down a staircase, and to the end of another catwalk.

"We've come to the end of the line," Fred said.

But nothing could keep Scooby from a Scooby Snack. He tied a rope to the end of the metal catwalk, swung to a door in the arena wall, and opened it. Daphne was inside.

"Good work, Scooby!" Fred said as Daphne and Scooby climbed back up the rope. "Are you okay, Daphne?"

"I'm just fine, Freddy," Daphne replied. "The Scary Skater dumped me in here and took off. I couldn't get out, or I'd have fallen."

"Good thing Scooby-Doo has a super sniffer that can smell a Scooby Snack anywhere," Shaggy said. Daphne pulled some Scooby Snacks out of her pocket and handed them to Scooby. "You wouldn't want to share a few of those, would you, pal?" Shaggy asked. Scooby gave him half, and the two of them munched happily.

"You know," Daphne said, "something peculiar happened when the Scary Skater and I were near the ceiling. I had some coins in my dress pocket and they all flew out and up."

"Interesting," Velma commented as they walked along the catwalk. They came to a staircase that led them back downstairs to the ice rink. As they walked past Icy's office, they saw the door was open. Inside, they noticed a diploma on the wall. "Icy has a degree in science," Velma noticed. "I wonder why he doesn't use it."

"Maybe he just likes running a skating arena," Fred suggested.

"I guess so," Daphne said. "He's got lots of pictures of himself skating with other famous skaters. They're all over the wall of this office." The gang peeked in and saw Icy on skates with many of the competitors who were skating in the championship.

The gang headed back to the rink. The competitors had started skating once again. By the edge of the rink, Icy was arguing with Los Korz. "I have every right to be here!" Los Korz shouted. "My nephew, Kenny, is skating, and I am here to cheer him on."

A thin young man in a skating suit

skated in from the ice. "It's okay, Uncle Los," he said. "You don't need to stay. I'll be all right."

"Kenny, I promised your mother I'd help in any way I could," Los Korz insisted. "And I'm staying."

"I wonder if his idea of helping includes shutting down the competition," Velma said. "Kenny can't lose if he doesn't compete."

"The same is true of Jenny Jumps," Daphne added.

"Icy or Kenny might have a reason to cause trouble, too," Fred said. "We just don't know what it is."

"I have a hunch about what's going on here," Velma said.

"Okay, then," Fred said to the gang. "I guess it's time to set a trap for that Scary Skater." They huddled and came up with a plan. When they were done, they hurried to the Mystery Machine. "I hope we can find what we need," Fred said as he took out the keys to the van. "Everything depends on it."

That night, the competitors were dressed in their costumes and ready to skate. Jenny Jumps skated around the inside edge of the rink, signing autographs. Los Korz's Kenny paced nervously, balanced on his skates. The many other skaters waited anxiously for their turns to skate.

The judges took their places right by the rink. Los Korz was seated behind them, though some of the judges didn't seem pleased about that. They sent him angry looks, but he ignored them.

When it was time for the competition to start, Icy Blades joined the gang at the inside edge of the rink. He was wearing skates. "I'm the master of ceremonies," he explained. "At least I get to skate a little." He pushed off into the center of the rink. "Welcome, ladies and gentlemen, to this year's Grand National Figure Skating Competition." He announced the order in which the skaters would compete, then skated off.

Jenny Jumps was the first skater out. She did a beautiful, graceful routine to a piece of classical music. She landed all her jumps perfectly. But, in the middle of her routine, the lights suddenly began to flicker and then turned off completely. A single spotlight lit the rink, and the Scary Skater was once again in the center of it.

Jenny screamed as the Scary Skater circled her, but she couldn't move from her spot. He scooped her up and was starting to rise. But as they rose off the ground, Jenny yanked at the Scary Skater's hair. She pulled out a metal bar and threw it to the ground.

Fred, Scooby, Velma, and Shaggy had skated onto the rink and stood below, holding a net. Jenny and the Scary Skater fell into it. Jenny bounced up and out while the gang wrapped the Scary Skater in the net.

The lights came on and the crowd clapped. Police made their way carefully onto the ice as Jenny Jumps pulled off a brown wig. It wasn't Jenny at all. It was Daphne, disguised as Jenny!

"And now let's find out who the Scary Skater really is," Fred said as he started to unwrap the net.

Do you know who the Scary Skater really was? Turn the page to find out if you're right.

"It's Icy Blades!" Daphne cried when Fred pulled off the man's mask.

"But why would he do this to his own arena?" one of the police officers asked.

"Because the skating world never appreciated my talent," Icy snarled angrily. "I bought this arena just so I could lure them all here and then ruin their competition."

"And you were able to do it because your knowledge of science taught you how to create a magnetic field under the ice," Velma added. "That's why the skaters couldn't move. Their steel ice skate blades were held down when Icy turned on the super-strong magnetic field."

Daphne reached into Icy's pocket and pulled out a small black box with a button. "He turned on the magnetic field under the ice with this remote control," she explained. "And then when he wanted to rise, he shut off the magnetic field below and turned on the one up there in that disco ball. The metal bar in his hat was what pulled him up to the giant magnet hidden in the disco ball."

"When I found the receipt for the disco ball and learned that it had just been installed, I suspected that something about it was important to this case," Velma said. "And I suspected magnetism when Scooby's dog tag was drawn to the ground and Daphne's change flew up into the air."

Fred held up his skate and revealed an odd-looking old-fashioned blade. All of the gang wore the same kind of skate. "Luckily, we found an antique dealer who had these old skates with wooden blades," he explained. "We weren't affected by the magnetism with these on."

"I've planned this for years," Icy said. "I wanted to be a famous skater. But I was ignored, so I fixed it so all eyes would be on me — in the spotlight at last. And I would have gotten away with it, too, if it wasn't for you meddling kids and your dog."

"Take a bow, Scooby!" Shaggy said.

Scooby spun on the ice and the crowd cheered. "Rooby-rooby-roo!" he shouted.

THE CASE OF THE
DREADFuL DRAGON

"**W**ow! What gorgeous boats!" Daphne said as she and the gang walked out onto the boat dock. "I'm glad we were able to rent one. Are you sure you know how to drive a power boat, Freddy?"

"I have my boat safety certificate right in my pocket," Fred assured her.

"It sure was nice of your uncle to invite us to this tropical island and let us stay at his house, Daphne," Velma said as she put on a pair of prescription sunglasses.

"Yeah, but what about the little mystery he wants us to solve?" Shaggy mentioned. "What tropical terrors await us?"

"Ropical rerrors," Scooby repeated with a fearful shiver.

"He just wants us to find out if anyone has been on his private island. He's too busy to go there very often, but people have been telling him that someone is on the island. If someone's there, we have to tell him or her to leave," Daphne explained.

They stopped in front of a sleek white powerboat. A man came out of the cabin. "Hello. I'm Shep Shipman, owner of the Speedy Boat Rental Company that rented this boat to you." He went over the paperwork with the gang and then gave them the keys. "Where are you going?" he asked.

"Dragon Island," Fred replied.

"You don't want to go there," Shep Shipman said. "There are treacherous winds, sharp reefs, and crosscurrents."

"Don't worry," Daphne said. "Freddy has his boat safety certificate with him. He'll know what to do."

"I'm warning you — don't go there," Shep Shipman insisted.

Several boats away from them, a loud argument broke out. The gang left Shep Shipman and hurried down the dock to see what was wrong. On the deck of a huge yacht, a man with glasses stood nose-to-nose with a gray-haired woman. They were yelling at one another. "You are not inviting all your business associates on this trip!" the woman shouted.

"This business trip is very important!" the man shouted back.

"But this is our fortieth anniversary!" the woman argued. As she spoke, a group of businesspeople walked down the dock. They bustled by and climbed onboard the yacht. The woman turned red with fury. She stormed off the yacht and onto the dock.

"Sorry, dear. I'll make it up to you," the man said as the yacht fired up its motors and pulled out of its dock slip.

"I'll get you back for this!" she yelled,

shaking her fist at him. He smiled and waved as the boat sped out of the marina.

"Is your husband Thornton G. Powell the third?" Velma asked. "I thought I recognized him from the business section of the newspaper."

"Why, yes. And I'm Muffy G. Powell," the woman replied.

"It's nice to meet you, Mrs. Powell," Fred said. "But we have to get going. We only have our boat for three hours." He and the gang headed back to their boat. On the way, Fred stopped to pick up a spool of kite string. "Someone dropped this," he said, putting it into his pocket.

Shep Shipman had left by the time they returned to the boat. "Ready to hit the high seas?" Fred asked as they all climbed aboard.

"Ready," Scooby said. He hung off the boat, slapping the water with a tennis racket in his paw.

The gang laughed as the water splashed them. "I didn't mean you really had to *hit* the sea," Fred explained. "It's only an expression, Scoob."

"Rorry," Scooby said, grinning.

Fred sat in the captain's chair and started the boat. Soon they were skimming over the crystal blue water. "I think that's Dragon Island," Daphne said, pointing to a green speck in the distance. "Head that way."

Fred turned the boat toward the island. The boat's speedometer climbed from 50 to 60 to 70 miles an hour. "Like, slow down, Fred," Shaggy suggested. "What's the hurry?"

"I'm trying," Fred told him. "But the boat keeps speeding up." The speedometer continued to climb — 80, 90, 100 miles per hour.

"Cut the motor!" Velma shouted. "We're about to crash into the island!"

Fred tried to turn the key, but it

wouldn't move. "It's jammed!" he cried as the boat hit a coral reef at 100 miles per hour. With the sound of shattering wood, the gang was tossed up high out of the boat. They fell under the water and came up gasping for air. "Swim for the island!" Fred shouted.

The gang began to swim. Scooby and Shaggy did the backstroke. But when they spotted a shark fin nearby, they both jumped up on scraps of floating boat wreckage and surfed. "Like, cow-abunga! Everyone out of the water!" Shaggy warned. "Shark attack!"

Fred, Daphne, and Velma doubled their swimming speed and soon collapsed on the shores of Dragon Island.

Scooby and Shaggy washed up right next to them. Scooby lay there, scared and exhausted. A tiny tropical fish that he'd accidentally swallowed popped out of his mouth.

"I always wondered what it would be like to be stranded on a deserted island,"

Velma said, shaking the water out of her hair.

"Let's look around and find out if it actually *is* deserted," Fred suggested.

They began to search the lush island, and discovered that it was full of tropical birds and flowers. After a little while, Velma stopped. "Where are Shaggy and Scooby?" she asked. "I haven't seen them for at least fifteen minutes." She noticed two hammocks made from vines swinging between palm trees. "Shaggy made these," Velma said. "I can tell from the way he tied the knots. They must have wanted to rest. Typical. But where are they now?"

"Look at these weird footprints," Daphne pointed out. "It looks like they were pulled out of the hammocks and dragged somewhere by some kind of creature."

"Let's follow the tracks," Fred suggested.

The tracks led them up the side of a mountain. "This is no ordinary mountain," Velma said. She pointed to a large, round hole in front of them. "It's a volcano — there's the opening."

"Gee, I hope it's not an active volcano," Daphne said.

"If you mean you hope it's not going to erupt and spew hot lava all over us, well, I don't know if it is or it isn't," Velma said. "But it sure is active. Listen." The three of them stuck their heads into the opening of the volcano. They heard metal clanking together inside.

"It sounds as if someone's building something down there," Fred said.

Before Daphne and Velma could reply, a twenty-foot dragon shot up out of the mouth of the volcano. It hovered over them, its mouth shooting fiery breath. "I am the ancient spirit of this island. You have angered me. Be gone!"

"Where are our friends?" Velma demanded.

"Leave, and they will be returned to you!" the voice boomed.

"Our boat is wrecked. We can't leave," Fred shouted.

"Your boat will appear!" the voice told them.

"Okay, we'll leave," Fred said.

"Very well!" the voice said. The dragon shot out a last blast of fire, then swirled in a circle and flew back down the volcano.

"We can't leave without Shaggy and Scooby," Daphne said.

"We won't," Fred replied. "I just want to see what will happen next." They walked back down the side of the volcano to the beach.

"Well, what do you know?" Velma said. Sitting out in the water was their boat, looking like new.

"We've got company," Daphne said, pointing.

The dragon appeared above the boat. "Go!" it bellowed as fire spurted from its mouth. "Go! Or you will never see your friends again!"

"We're going! We're going!" Velma said as the three of them plunged into the surf. They swam out to the boat and climbed onboard. Instantly, they heard movement in the cabin. Something banged against the door.

The door flew open and Shaggy and Scooby tumbled out. They were tied and gagged. Fred and Daphne quickly freed them. "What happened?" Velma asked.

"Scoob and I were taking a little snooze when four creatures came and dragged us out of our comfy hammocks," Shaggy explained.

"What did they look like?" Daphne asked.

"They were about ten feet tall and they looked like big lizards," Shaggy said.

Scooby nodded. "Rig rizards."

"Like dragons?" Velma asked.

"Exactly," Shaggy agreed.

"This can't possibly be the same boat we came here in," Daphne said. "But how could someone come up with an- other boat so quickly?"

"I guess they rented it," Velma said as she came out of the boat's cabin. She held up a pad she'd found in there. It had the name and address of Speedy Rentals on the letterhead. "I found this pad and some parasailing equipment in a closet in there," she said. She examined the top of the pad. "Someone wrote a note on the page above this sheet of paper," she ob- served. "It left an impression on the page below it. Does anyone have a pencil?"

"I have a makeup pencil," Daphne of- fered as she reached into her pocket for it.

"That will do," Velma said, taking it from her. Using the side of the pencil, she colored the entire page. That caused the writing that had been written on the page above it to show more clearly. "'The space is nearly done,'" Velma read the note. "'Come see it today. S.'"

Daphne held up her hand to shield her eyes from the sun as she looked out onto the horizon. "There's that yacht Mr. Powell took his business associates out on," she observed. "They seem to be coming this way."

Fred rubbed his cheek thoughtfully. "I think it's time to set a trap," he said. "Shaggy, you've parasailed before, haven't you?"

"You mean that sport where a person flies in the air under a big sail while a powerboat tows you at top speed?" Shaggy asked.

"That's the one," Fred said.

"No. I'm not doing it. No way. No how," Shaggy insisted.

"Ro ray. Ro row," Scooby agreed.

"I have a box of Scooby Snacks back at the house," Daphne mentioned.

Scooby and Shaggy looked at one another. "I'm always up for a new challenge," Shaggy said. "How about you, Scoob?"

"Rokay," Scooby agreed.

"Great!" Fred said. "Here's my plan."

Fred drove the boat very slowly. All the while, he played the onboard radio as loudly as it would go. Velma and Daphne sat at the front of the boat, telling jokes and laughing. They drove back and forth in front of the volcano, hoping to be noticed.

Shaggy and Scooby waited on the beach. They were strapped into a double harness, with Scooby sitting in front of Shaggy. They watched the boat go back and forth.

As the gang had hoped, the dragon rose up out of the opening in the volcano. "You should not still be here!" the voice around it boomed. "I will send my servants to destroy you!" A door opened at the base of the volcano and twelve tall dragon-men on wave runners zoomed out.

Fred drove the boat close to shore and

tossed a rope with a clip on the end to Shaggy. Shaggy clipped it to the harness as Fred zoomed away in the boat. In seconds, Shaggy and Scooby were rising into the air, towed by the boat. Shaggy held tight to Scooby. "Like, are those snapping turtles I hear or is it the sound of my teeth chattering?" he asked nervously.

"Rour reeth rattering," Scooby replied.

The dragon's wave runners quickly surrounded the boat. Fred spun in a circle, creating a big wave. The dragon-men tumbled from their wave runners as the wave washed over them.

"Whoa! Whoa! Whoa!" Shaggy shouted. The circling boat was spinning the parasail around, too. Scooby and Shaggy spun so fast that it made them dizzy.

"Shaggy, get the big dragon!" Daphne shouted. Fred straightened his course and drove the boat right into the dragon. Scooby and Shaggy were up in the air at the same height as the dragon. "Use the string!" Fred shouted.

Shaggy reached into his pocket and took out the kite string Fred had found on the dock. He twirled it in the air and hurled it at the dragon. The string circled the dragon, wrapping all around it.

The dragon spurted a blast of fire, but Fred revved the engine and sped away, pulling Shaggy and Scooby with him. The dragon seemed to chase them because Shaggy still held the kite string and was pulling it along. When Fred slowed down, Shaggy and Scooby descended onto the beach, dragging the dragon with them. Shaggy undid his harness and began following the string he still held in his hand. It seemed to lead toward a patch of tropical shrubbery.

Suddenly, a dragon-man ran out from the shrubbery. "Get him, Scoob!" Shaggy cried. Scooby-Doo chased the dragon-man, still pulling the parasail behind him. Pouncing, he knocked down the dragon-man and held him pinned to the ground.

The rest of the gang swam ashore, soon catching up to Scooby. "Good job, Scooby," Daphne said. "That dragon was just a big kite, and now you've caught the person flying it."

Fred reached down to the struggling dragon-man under Scooby and took hold of the dragon mask. "Let's see who this kite master is."

Do you know who's under the mask? See the next page to find out if you're right.

"Shep Shipman!" Daphne cried. "But why?"

Scooby climbed off Shep Shipman and let him sit up. "I was going to make a fortune by selling this deserted island to Thornton G. Powell the third," he grumbled.

"But my uncle owns this island," Daphne told him.

"Who cares? He never comes here. If I could keep other people away from the island, he'd never know," Shep Shipman said. "I've already built Mr. Powell a secret laboratory down in the volcano where he could develop new products, and I was going to provide him with a private security force."

"Your dragon-men?" Fred asked.

Shep Shipman nodded. Thornton Powell's yacht pulled up to the shore, and the gang turned to see the billionaire and his business associates use a plank to get off the boat and onto the beach. "Shipman, why are you wearing that ridiculous dragon outfit?" Thornton Powell demanded to know.

"Mr. Shipman was planning to sell you some property he doesn't own," Daphne informed him.

"I would have gotten away with it, too, if it weren't for you meddling kids," Shep Shipman snapped.

"Hey, like, where is Scooby-Doo?" Shaggy asked.

"He's really been blown away by this case," Velma joked. She pointed into the sky where Scooby floated on the parasail, blown there by a sudden gust of wind.

"Rooby-rooby-roo!" he shouted.

THE CASE OF THE SKATEBOARDING SCAM

"Dudes! Watch out!" called a young man in baggy pants, dark sunglasses, and a red baseball cap as he whizzed by Fred, Velma, and Daphne.

"Jinkies! These skateboarders go so fast! I can't understand how they stay on those things!" Velma cried, stepping quickly out of the path of still more zooming skateboarders. She watched the skaters zipping up and down ramps and doing all sorts of tricks.

"They're incredible," said Daphne. Fred nodded in agreement.

Scooby and Shaggy had left earlier in search of skateboards, knee pads, and helmets to rent so they could try out the course for themselves. Now they returned, ready to go. "Like, we are ready to roll," Shaggy announced.

"Ready ro roll," Scooby agreed.

A woman in khaki boarding pants, a black tank top, and a pair of beaten-up skateboarding shoes rode up to Fred, Daphne, and Velma. She stepped hard on the tail of the skateboard, flipping it up into her arms as she dismounted. Taking off her black, sticker-covered helmet, she tucked a strand of short, neon-pink hair behind her ear and smiled happily. "Fred! I see you got the invitations to come watch the skateboarding competition!" she cried, hugging Fred.

"Yeah! Thanks for sending them!" Fred said. He turned to face the slightly confused Daphne and Velma. "This is Alicia, my cousin from San Francisco."

"Pleased to meet you!" Alicia said with a smile. "I'm in a big invitation-only skateboarding competition here in Los Angeles.

I wanted Fred and his friends to be able to get in. I'm really nervous because I'm competing against Boney Squawk! Almost no one can beat him!"

"I'm sure you'll do great, Alicia," Fred said. "You've won a whole bunch of competitions before."

As the gang stood talking with Alicia, a man on a neon-orange skateboard with blue tinted see-through wheels, golden trucks, and red grip tape skated into the park. Everyone turned and whispered. "Zoinks! That's Boney Squawk!" Shaggy shouted excitedly.

"Who?" Daphne asked.

"He's a skating champion who owns one of the most expensive skateboards ever made," Fred explained. "It was designed especially for him by a major skateboard company."

Suddenly, a loud yelp and a crash came from the skate park. "Scoob!" Shaggy yelled as he hurried over to Scooby, who was whimpering and clutching his tail. Velma, Fred, and Daphne followed him.

"What happened?" Velma asked as she knelt down next to Scooby to examine his tail. Scooby howled loudly at her touch.

"I'm so sorry!" said the person who had run over Scooby's tail. It was none other than Boney Squawk himself!

"What happened?" Alicia asked. She skated up next to Scooby with a first aid kit.

"Well, that big dog had fallen off of his board and was lying on the ground. I had just jumped the fly box, and when I landed — it happened to be on his tail." Boney explained. "I'm sorry."

Boney Squawk went to pick up his skateboard, but just then, a figure zoomed by on a black skateboard. It wore a flowing black cloak and a big white mask that covered its entire head. The gang, Alicia, and Boney Squawk all looked up just in time to see the figure grab Boney's prized skateboard before zipping away.

"Come back here!" Boney cried. "Can I borrow your skateboard?" he asked Alicia.

"I'd be honored!" Alicia replied. Boney nodded and took off after the figure. He chased it to the parking lot, in and out of the parked cars. He seemed to catch up to it, but then the figure disappeared — with the skateboard!

"No!" Boney yelled, slamming down his helmet furiously. "I can't skate without my lucky board! What am I going to do?"

Alicia and the gang ran up to Boney Squawk. "Maybe we can help, Boney," Fred offered.

Boney turned around slowly. "How?" he asked.

"We're Mystery, Inc.!" Velma cried. "Solving cases like this is what we do."

"Thanks," Boney said. "It's worth a try."

"Let's get cracking then!" Fred said. He headed back to the scene of the crime. The gang and Alicia followed, with Boney bringing up the rear. As they walked back into the skate park, a girl in black jeans and blue-streaked hair glared at them.

"Good thing Boney Squawk can't skate now! Reis Ziggy is a better skater anyway!" she yelled.

"Who is Reis Ziggy?" Daphne asked the gang.

"He's Boney's arch rival. He always comes in second place while Boney comes in first," Alicia said.

"Yeah, if Boney didn't compete, then Reis Ziggy would have a really good chance of winning," Shaggy added.

Daphne walked over to the girl who had yelled at them. She looked at her T-shirt, which had a picture of Reis Ziggy on it. It showed him midair, going over a jump. "You're a Reis Ziggy fan, I see," Daphne said.

"Of course! He's better than Boney Squawk and deserves to win!" the girl said. "I'm Juliet Maltski, Reis's girlfriend. It's good to meet another Reis Ziggy fan!"

"Well, not really but . . ." Daphne began to say.

"Not a fan? Then get out of my face." Juliet cut her off. She sneered at Daphne and walked away.

Daphne shook her head and returned to the gang. "I think I found a good suspect — Juliet Maltski. She's a really big fan of Reis Ziggy and seems like she would do anything to help Reis win."

"Dudes! Watch out!" The skater in the red baseball cap yelled again. He tumbled to the pavement to avoid crashing into the gang and Alicia.

"Jeepers! Sorry! We shouldn't be standing in the middle of a busy skate park," Daphne said, bending over to help the skater up to his feet. "Are you all right?"

"Yeah, I think so." His sunglasses had

fallen off and Daphne looked into his eyes for a moment before he quickly put them back on. "My name's Danny Vasquez," he said. "I've come to see the competition. Can I ask why you guys are just standing here?"

"We're looking for Boney Squawk's stolen skateboard." Shaggy said. Scooby nodded and held onto his tail to make sure another skateboarder didn't run it over again.

"Dude! You know Boney Squawk? That's *so* cool!" Danny cried loudly. "Man, I'd do anything for a skateboard like his. Anything! It's so awesome!"

The gang looked at one another with suspicious raised eyebrows. Alicia nodded. "Right, well, we'd better keep looking, guys." Alicia said, then looked to Danny. "Nice to meet you."

"Right on, man." Danny said. As the gang began to walk away, he took off his red baseball cap as if in salute.

"I suppose we should follow the path

the villain took?" Fred suggested to the group. They all nodded and turned around to face the direction from which the thief had come. Looking through rows upon rows of parked cars was tiring, but they kept going. Finally they came to a green car with the license plate BONEYSGRL.

"I'm guessing this is Amanda's car." Alicia said.

"Who is Amanda?" Fred asked.

"Boney's girlfriend. See?" At this, she pointed to the license plate. "Her name is Amanda DeMala."

"That name sounds really familiar." Velma said slowly, beginning to make her way over to the Mystery Machine. Fred, Daphne, Shaggy, Scooby, and Alicia stayed to examine the car.

"Ah, ha!" Velma cried from the van, moments later. "I knew I recognized her name! Come look at what I found, you guys!" The gang and Alicia walked over to the Mystery Machine and peered inside. Velma had her laptop open to a news web page. "I located an interview I read a while back about Amanda De-Mala. In the interview, she talked about how she didn't like the idea of Boney skateboarding because it was too dangerous. She would prefer it if he went into some other profession." Velma looked up from the screen. "Do you think she'd do this to her own boyfriend?"

"I don't know. But we found a large black cloak on the ground under her car," Daphne said, showing Velma the cloak.

"We should go talk to her," Fred said. Everyone nodded, and Velma showed them a picture of Amanda DeMala from the Internet. After about a half hour of searching, they found her at the skate park.

Amanda was tall with shoulder-length platinum blond hair that was angled about her slim face. She wore a red T-shirt and a pair of jeans. A red paisley bandanna covered her right wrist. She sat on a bench under the shade of a large maple tree and looked up at the small crowd approaching her.

"Hi," Fred said. "We're trying to help Boney find his skateboard. We want to know how you feel about Boney's skate-boarding."

Amanda rolled here eyes. "He's going to get really hurt one of these days," she answered. "But I can't stop him."

Velma noticed Amanda's wrist and the tightly wrapped bandanna that covered it. "What happened to your wrist?" Velma asked politely.

"None of your business," she said. "But I did it skateboarding."

"You don't skateboard," Alicia challenged her.

As an answer, Amanda grabbed her skateboard and helmet from the ground and walked off toward the skate park. The gang followed her. She strapped on her helmet, mounted the skateboard, and began showing some of her best tricks.

Juliet Maltski walked by and saw her skating. "Reis Ziggy rules!" she shouted at Amanda.

"I think it's time to make a plan," Velma suggested.

Scooby and Shaggy whizzed by Velma, Fred, and Daphne on their skateboards. "I assume you'll be needing someone to get the villain's attention," Shaggy said.

"Well . . . yes," Fred admitted. "We usually do."

"This time, we don't mind. We'd do anything for Boney," Shaggy said.

Shaggy and Scooby skated back and forth in the skate park. They each rode identical copies of the Boney Squawk skateboard that had been taken. The gang had created the fakes with spray paint and decals they'd bought at a hardware store.

The cloaked figure suddenly appeared in the park. It did several spectacular jumps — and then went after Scooby and

Shaggy. They jumped high into the air and spun their boards, but the cloaked figure stayed right on them. Just when it seemed ready to reach out and grab their boards, Fred, Daphne, and Velma stepped out from the side of the park and tossed a net at it.

Tangled in the net, the mystery skater shouted in frustration. "Now let's see who we've snagged," Fred said.

Do you think you know who the mystery skater is? Turn the page to see if you're right.

"**I**t's Danny Vasquez," Daphne said as Fred untangled the net.

"No!" Velma disagreed. She removed his red baseball cap and dark sunglasses. "It's really Reis Ziggy. He disguised himself because he wanted it to appear as if he hadn't arrived yet. But the fact that Juliet Maltski, his girlfriend, was here made me suspicious."

"I saw a picture of Reis on her T-shirt. When Danny Vasquez's sunglasses fell off, I knew it was Reis Ziggy," Daphne said.

"We suspected Amanda DeMala, but when we saw her skateboarding, we realized that she just wasn't as good as the cloaked skateboarder had been," Fred went on. "She even wore a bandanna to disguise an injury. Reis might have thrown the cloak under her car to make us think she was the culprit, or maybe he just dropped it."

"I'm sick of losing to Boney!" Reis snarled. "If it weren't for him, I'd be the number one skater in the country. And I'd have won this competition if it weren't for you kids and your dog."

"Maybe not," said Shaggy, kicking his board high into the air and catching it again. "You haven't seen Scoob and me skate yet."

Scooby skated off a ramp and spun on the end of his tail. "Rooby-rooby-roo!" he cried.

"White-water rafting! What a thrill!" Fred said, buckling on his helmet. The gang stood on the bank of a rushing river, ready for a raft ride. They all wore helmets and life vests, and carried paddles.

A woman in a life vest and helmet stepped out of the nearby woods and joined them. "I hope all of you are enjoying yourselves," the woman said to the gang. "My name is Cindy Slicker, and my husband owns this company, River Runs."

"Wow! Like, what a cool job," said Shaggy.

Cindy shrugged. "Heaven knows my husband loves taking these trips, but

I'm a city person. Two years ago, he told me were just taking a little vacation out here. Then he bought this river rafting company, and we never went back to the city. There's no theater, no fashionable stores, and no good restaurants out here. Horrible!"

The leader of the trip, Harry Slicker, joined them. "Ready for a great adventure?" he asked them. "Any questions?"

"Like, what time is lunch served?" Shaggy asked.

"Any time you get the chance to eat it," he said. "It's in this waterproof carrying case, but I can't promise it won't get wet. Everything gets wet on these trips."

A large man dressed in rafting gear approached them. He led five other people, also dressed for rafting. "Are you giving them the speech about how they're going to get wet, Harry?"

"Go away, Thor," Harry said.

Thor laughed a loud belly laugh. "Folks, if you don't want to get soaked, come join us on River Ways Tours. I actually know something about white-water rafting, unlike Harry here."

"You should listen to him, Harry," Cindy Slicker said. "He was born out here in this part of the world. We're city people. We should leave this stuff to people like Thor Thorbert who know how to do it."

"I know what I'm doing, Cindy," Harry insisted. He turned to Thor Thorbert. "Please take your people and get lost, Thor."

Thor Thorbert chuckled and continued to lead his group onto a large orange raft on the bank. "So long, you soon-to-be-soaked suckers!" Thor called to them.

"Ignore him," Harry told them. "Let's go!" They all climbed into their own orange raft and Harry shoved off.

"This isn't so hard," Velma said as they all started paddling down the river.

"Wait," Cindy Slicker said. "This is the

easy part." Soon they came to a part of the river where the water began to swirl around huge rocks. White foam splashed up and sprayed their faces.

"I'm working up an appetite, Scoob," Shaggy said. "I hope there's a restaurant at the end of this river."

"Reah, restaurant," Scooby agreed.

"Don't count on it," Cindy Slicker said.

Suddenly, the raft began to spin, caught in a whirlpool. "What's that in the water?" Daphne yelled, pointing at two brown mounds rising up by the raft.

"They're just rocks," Harry told her.

"No, they're not," Velma cried. "They're furry!"

The rocks rose higher and higher. Then, all at once, a giant rat rose up from the water in front of them. It chattered with long, sharp teeth and began grabbing for the raft.

"Like, stroke!" Shaggy yelled. But as hard as they paddled they didn't seem to be getting anywhere. The rat batted at them with its paws, and they swatted back at it with their paddles.

"I know what to do!" Shaggy yelled. He spun Scooby's tail in a circle until it was coiled tightly. Then he sat Scooby at the back of the raft with his tail dragging in the water and let it uncoil. Scooby's tail spun like an eggbeater and made a kind of motor. The raft sped forward and away from the river rat. "Way to go, Scooby!" Shaggy cheered.

"What was that thing?" Daphne asked Harry. "Have you seen it before?"

"Well, yes," Harry admitted. "It had appeared on the last several trips I've taken."

"I think I saw something like that on *Chiller Movies* last night," Shaggy said. "It escaped from a laboratory after being exposed to radioactivity."

Harry pulled the raft over to the shore. "We should all chill out and have some lunch," he said. They sat on the shore and ate their lunches out of bags.

A piece of paper blew past Fred, and he grabbed it. "Harryland Amusement Park," he read. Daphne and Velma looked over his shoulder. The paper showed plans for rides and various characters.

"It must have fallen out of Harry's pack," Velma said, noticing that the pack was open. Scooby began pulling something from the pack. Velma got up from her rock and took it from him. It was a bundle of red, yellow, and green wires. "Harry," she said. "Do we travel back the same way we came?"

"No, we go in a circle that loops back to where we saw the river rat," he answered

"Is the river rat usually still there?" she asked.

"Always," he told her.

Velma sat back down with Fred, Daphne, Scooby, and Shaggy.

"Are you thinking we need a plan, Velma?" Fred asked.

She nodded and took a waterproof bag

of Scooby Snacks from her pocket. "It's a good thing I came prepared," she said, "because we're going to need Scooby's and Shaggy's help."

After lunch, Harry, Cindy, and the gang climbed into the raft for the trip back. Soon, the river looped into the section where they'd seen the rat. As Harry had said, the river rat began to rise once again. It rocked the boat. Its deafening chatter was terrifying.

Just as the gang had planned, Scooby and Shaggy jumped out of the raft and onto a flat boulder that jutted from the river. They each brought a long rope with them. "Hey, rat!" Shaggy shouted.

"Rey, rat!" Scooby repeated.

The rat slowly turned and slogged through the water toward them. Scooby and Shaggy tied their ropes into lassos and twirled them a few times before throwing them over the rat's head.

Sparks flew as the electronic rat's head hit the water.

"No!" cried the person who had built the rat and put it there in the first place.

Do you think you know who put the river rat in the river. Turn the page to find out if you're right.

"**H**arry!" Cindy Slicker cried. "Is this one of your creations?"

Harry sat down in the raft and nodded sadly. "I wanted to sell the rafting company and open my own amusement park," he admitted as the river carried them along. "You're right, Thor Thorbert is much better at this than I am, and the company was losing money. But I didn't want everyone to think I'd failed. So I tested out one of the robotic animals I was planning on making for my amusement park and planted it in the river."

"When we saw your plans, we had our first clue," Fred said.

"And when Scooby pulled some wiring from your bag, we put it together," Velma added.

"Does this mean we're going back to the city?" Cindy asked.

"Yes," Harry told her. "Do you mind?"

Cindy Slicker smiled brightly. "Oh, Harry!" she cried as she threw her arms around his neck. Her sudden motion caused the raft to flip, tossing them all into the water.

One by one, each of the gang came up for air. Scooby spit out a small fountain of river water from his mouth. "Rooby-rooby-roo!" he cheered.

"**I** can't believe I've finally made it to Broadway!" Velma cried. She spread her arms wide and twirled excitedly. She and the gang were on a street corner in New York City, at the center of the city's theater district.

"Look at all these signs for plays," Daphne said. "I want to see all of them!"

"We have to go see Jane Rich at the Bluebird Theater," Fred reminded them. "She says she's got a problem that she needs help with." They walked down the busy city street, past several theaters, until they arrived at the Bluebird.

A big marquee sign over the front doors read: JANE RICH IN *MY WORLD*. "It's all about her life in musical theater, and it's a big hit," Daphne explained. "But lately there's been a problem with the show."

They went into the lobby where Jane Rich was already waiting for them. She was a tall, blond woman in her sixties with a throaty, full voice. "Darlings!" she greeted them. "I'm so thrilled you're finally here. I read about your other cases in the paper and knew that if anyone could help me, it was Mystery, Inc. Heaven knows I don't want to bring the police into this. That would be terrible publicity for the show — which is completely sold out, by the way."

"What's the problem, Ms. Rich?" Fred asked.

"It would be better if you saw for yourself," she said. "The Saturday matinee starts in an hour. Sit and watch the show as my guests."

"Super!" Velma said. "This will be my first Broadway show. They don't have much theater back home in Coolsville."

Since the show didn't start for an hour, the theater was still empty. Jane Rich directed the gang to front-row seats and then went backstage to get ready. After about five minutes, a man in a sweater and slacks sat down near them. He began sneezing violently.

"That's the theater critic, Frank Grumbles," Daphne told the gang. "He writes reviews of all the Broadway plays."

Frank Grumbles glanced at them and raised an eyebrow. "Pardon me, but is that a *dog* I see sitting there? Since when are *dogs* allowed in the theater?"

"He may look like a dog — and act like a dog and bark like a dog — but he's really not a dog," Shaggy replied.

"Oh?" Frank Grumbles said. "What is he?"

"An ace detective," Shaggy said.

"An ace detective *dog*," the critic insisted. "That means he does *not* belong in a theater."

"Scoob goes where I go," Shaggy argued.

"Then I suggest you both leave," Frank Grumbles said as he took a handkerchief from his pocket and began sneezing again.

"Frank, don't be such a pain," Jane Rich said, peeking her head out from behind the curtain. "The young man and his dog can come up here and watch the show from backstage. Does that suit you?"

"As long as it's far enough away from me that my allergies aren't set off," Frank Grumbles agreed grumpily.

"I didn't know dogs bothered you, Frank," Jane Rich said.

"There's a lot you don't know," Frank Grumbles snapped at her. Shaggy and Scooby shot him dark looks as they climbed the side stairs up to the stage and disappeared behind the curtain with Jane Rich.

"That's a good place for them to sit,"

Daphne said. "Maybe they'll see something from there that we'd miss from down here."

Suddenly, a woman began shouting. "No way! I am not standing here with a giant dog! Forget it!" A young, blond woman ran out from the theater wings. She looked a lot like Jane Rich, only much younger.

Shaggy hurried out after her. "But everybody loves Scooby," he said to her. "You would, too, if you got to know him."

"I have more important things to do then befriend a Great Dane," she snapped. "I am Ms. Rich's understudy, Ima Star. If she can't go on stage for any reason, I star in the play for her. I have to remember all her lines."

"How exciting!" Velma cried.

Ima Star shook her head. "Believe me, it's not. Jane Rich never misses a performance. I've never gone on. Night after night, I stand in the wings and memorize her lines, but I've never played the role onstage."

"Maybe you could stand on the other side of the theater since you don't like dogs," Daphne suggested.

"Oh, all right!" Ima Star agreed angrily, and she stomped off to the opposite side of the stage.

With a wave, Shaggy rejoined Scooby behind the curtain in the wings. Soon the audience arrived, and the show began. Jane Rich came out and told some jokes. She sang a few songs, and everything was going well.

Then, suddenly, all the lights went out. The audience was plunged into complete darkness. When the lights came on again, Jane Rich was tied and gagged. In the center stage was a clown with a scary, menacing grin. His legs were ten feet long, and he hopped around easily, doing a dance. He sang "Give My Regards to Broadway" in a deep, loud voice. "I am the

Broadway Bounder!" he announced when his song was done. "I am the spirit of the theater. I appear whenever a show stinks!"

The audience sat there, stunned. But then a loud, piercing whistle sounded. It was painful to listen to, and the audience ran from the theater with their hands over their ears. The lights turned off again, and the crowd panicked in the dark as they bumped into chairs and one another in their rush to escape the shrill blast.

When the audience was gone, the lights came back on. The Broadway Bounder had completely disappeared. Fred leaped onstage and untied Jane Rich. "Are you all right?" he asked.

"No," Jane Rich replied. "I twisted my ankle trying to get away from that Broadway Bounder. I can't even stand on it now."

Ima Star ran out from the wings. "Don't worry, Ms. Rich," she said. "I'll take over for you. I know all the lines."

"No, you won't," said a man who walked across the stage toward them. "I'm closing down this show."

"This is Donald Maverick, the Broadway producer," Jane introduced the gang to the man. "He's the fella who provides the money to put on this show. Donald, you've wanted to close my show from the start."

"That's because it's been losing money right from the start," he said. "I don't know why you won't let me charge more for a ticket. At least the show was a hit, but now, with this crazy character deafening people at every show, people will start demanding their money back."

"I want to keep the tickets reasonably priced," Jane Rich explained. "I don't think it's fair that only the wealthy should be able to see a Broadway play."

"Can we take a look around the theater?" Fred requested.

"I wonder if Scooby and Shaggy saw anything unusual," Daphne said. She looked around for them, but they weren't there. "Now where did they go?"

Something started thumping and banging. "It's coming from under the stage," Fred said. He ran and pulled open a trap door.

"Zoinks!" Shaggy cried as his head popped up. "That Broadway Bounder stuck us down here just before he went onstage," he reported. "I've heard of being stage struck, but we were stage *stuck!*"

Fred helped them up, and they joined the others in searching the theater. On the walls of the lobby, newspaper articles about different Broadway plays were framed and hanging on the walls. "Check this out," Shaggy said. "It's a review of the musical, *Dogs!* written by Frank Grumbles. He sure made it seem as if he likes dogs here." The picture with the article showed the critic sitting with a lot of dogs. He was smiling and petting them.

They searched the lobby some more, then went backstage. When they got to

Jane Rich's dressing room, they found the star in it, relaxing with her foot up on a stool.

"What's this, Ms. Rich?" Velma asked. She had picked a play by Frank Grumbles off the floor. It was titled, *Tent: A Story of a Circus*.

"Oh, it's a play Frank wrote and wanted me to star in," Jane Rich answered. "It's awful, and I told him so."

Ima Star came into the dressing room wearing the same outfit Jane Rich had worn onstage. "I've convinced Mr. Maverick to keep the show open tonight for the evening performance," she said excitedly. "I'll be in it. I'm going to invite every journalist and critic in the city to come see me!"

"Ima, aren't you worried about the Broadway Bounder ruining your performance?" Velma asked.

Ima shrugged and shook her head. "I'm just an optimist," she replied. "I have a feeling everything will be fine."

"Lucky you," Jane Rich said grimly, rubbing her twisted ankle. "I was tired of performing every night, anyway. I needed a rest."

"Speaking of rest," Daphne said. "I think we should go back to our hotel rooms and rest before the show tonight."

"Good idea," Velma agreed. "It will give me time to do some Internet research on my laptop."

The kids returned to the hotel and met in the room Velma and Daphne were sharing. Velma immediately opened her laptop and started typing in the names of all the people involved with the case.

Shaggy phoned room service. "We'll have ten of those shrimp cocktails," he ordered, "and ten hot fudge sundaes. I'm having a little get-together." He hung up and snickered mischievously. "Scooby and I are going to get all the food together and eat it!"

"I found a newspaper article written by Malcolm Grumbles," Velma reported.

"Listen to this title, 'The Legend of the Broadway Bounder.' It describes a character just like the one who's been appearing."

"Do you think Frank Grumbles could have written it under a fake name?" Daphne asked.

"Maybe," Velma replied.

"It couldn't be Frank Grumbles," Shaggy said as he went to the door to get his room service order. "When that Broadway Bounder stuck us under the stage, he wasn't sneezing."

"And he was in the audience the whole time," Fred added.

"I'm reading his play, *Tent*," Daphne said as she turned a page of the manuscript she'd taken from Jane Rich's dressing room. "It seems that Frank Grumbles knows a lot about circus life."

"The Broadway Bounder could be Donald Maverick. He wanted to close the show, which was losing money even though he'd sold all the tickets," Fred said. "And it could be Ima Star, who might have wanted something to happen to Jane Rich so she could go on."

"She did seem strangely sure that nothing would happen during the show tonight," Velma recalled.

"I think our best bet is to set a trap at the show tonight," Fred suggested. He looked at Shaggy and Scooby.

"I know! I know!" Shaggy said. "Get ready, Scoob. I have a feeling we're going to be appearing on Broadway very soon."

That night, the theater was packed. All the reporters Ima Star had invited were there, along with the regular sold-out audience. "Frank Grumbles and Donald Maverick are both in the audience," Daphne reported as she peeked out of the curtain from the stage. The gang had gotten permission to stay backstage and keep watch for the Broadway Bounder.

"I hope you know we feel ridiculous,"

Shaggy complained. He and Scooby were dressed in big hoop skirts and bonnets.

"They're the only costumes we could find for you," Daphne said.

Soon it was time for the show to start. The curtain went up and Ima Star came out on stage.

Five minutes into the show, the lights went off. When they turned back on, Ima Star was tied up at the side of the stage and the Broadway Bounder was once again leaping around the stage singing "Give My Regards to Broadway."

Suddenly, Scooby and Shaggy tap-danced out onto the stage in front of the Broadway Bounder. As the gang had hoped, this made the Bounder furious. He stopped singing and stomped toward them angrily.

The gang had stretched a rope across the stage. When the Broadway Bounder stepped, Fred pulled the end on one side and Daphne pulled her end from the other side of the stage. The Bounder collapsed. Its pants slid down, revealing two tall stilts.

"Now let's see who's under this mask," Fred said as he ran onto the stage and grabbed the Broadway Bounder's mask.

Do you think you know who's under the Broadway Bounder's mask? If so, look at the next page and find out if you're right!

"**L**ike, it's Frank Grumbles!" Shaggy shouted when Fred lifted off the Broadway Bounder's mask.

The theater critic shook his fist at the gang. "You shouldn't have stopped me! Someone needed to show Jane Rich that she wasn't the only one who could be a success on Broadway. I wrote a wonderful review of this play, and then she went and said that my play wasn't any good. I vowed to get revenge."

"But how did he manage to be in the audience and on the stage?" Jane Rich asked as she hobbled onto the stage on crutches.

"The man in the audience is Malcolm Grumbles, Frank's twin brother," Velma explained. "We knew there must be two of them. The man in the audience was allergic to Scooby, but the Broadway Bounder didn't sneeze at all when he was near him."

"Malcolm thought he was covering for me so that I could take a vacation," Frank said. "He's been interested in the story of the Broadway Bounder all his life. I took the idea from him, but he has no idea I was the one up on stage impersonating the Bounder."

"Frank knew how to walk on stilts because he was a circus clown before becoming a theater critic," Daphne informed them. "His play, *Tent,* is all about his experiences as a circus performer."

Donald Maverick joined them. "I know you wanted to ruin the show, Grumbles, but you've made it the talk of the town. Everyone wants to come and see the Broadway Bounder. I'd like to work on a scene where you and Jane sing a song together."

"You mean he and Ima," Jane said. "I'll be busy rehearsing for my new one-woman, one-dog-show. It will star Scooby and me, and I'll call it, *Scooby and Me: A Great Dane and a Great Dame.*"

Scooby seemed to like the idea. "Rooby-rooby-roo!" he shouted.